The Hands of Innocence

He cursed as he pumped the accelerator up and down without effect and the engine seemed to be about to die.

She began to wind down the window, without any clear idea of what she intended to do. He took his left hand off the steering-wheel and swept it round, hitting her in the throat. Pain streaked through her neck and she choked violently.

For several seconds, while her mind was shocked, she tried to overcome the agony in her throat. When that had eased a bit she realized the car had stopped and that the man had turned round sideways and was looking at her. An oncoming car's headlights filled the interior of the car with light and she could see his face, under the peaked cap, quite clearly. The eyes now seemed to be wild: almost mad were the words that occurred to her. The face suddenly became frighteningly familiar. Even though he was in uniform, this was Krammer, the man who had escaped from jail.

Her bewildered mind told her that she had to escape, no matter what. No one in her form at school really knew what this man had done to those girls he had killed, but they had gone through all the possibilities that occurred to them and had frightened themselves with the horrible things they thought up.

Other titles in the Walker British Mystery Series

JEFFREY
ASHFORD

The
Hands
of
Innocence

WALKER AND COMPANY · NEW YORK

Copyright © John Long Limited 1965

All rights reserved. No part of this book may be
reproduced or transmitted in any form or by any
means, electric or mechanical, including photocopying,
recording, or by any information storage and retrieval
system, without permission in writing from the Publisher.

All the characters and events portrayed in this story
are fictitious.

First published in the United States of America
in 1966 by the Walker Publishing Company, Inc.

This paperback edition first published in 1984.

ISBN: 0-8027-3049-3

Library of Congress Catalog Card Number: 66-12660

Printed in the United States of America

10 9 8 7 6 5 4 3 2 1

One

'Members of the jury, you have heard all the evidence and counsel have addressed you in their closing speeches. It is now my duty to sum up, to remind you of the evidence, and to tell you the law. I am the judge of the law, you are the judges of the facts. When I tell you what the law is you have to accept what I say, but should I suggest to you what interpretation may be placed on certain facts you are at complete liberty to accept or reject what I say.

'This is a trial for capital murder. As you have been told, the law of homicide was changed in nineteen hundred and fifty-seven when the crime of capital murder—that is, murder for which the punishment is judicial hanging— was introduced and differentiated from non-capital murder. George Krammer has been charged with two separate murders and you must try him on this charge of capital murder. You are not at liberty to argue about, or to take into account, the so-called morality of capital punishment, nor may you take any note whatsoever of the declared intention of the government to pass an Act abolishing all capital punishment. If you decide the prisoner was guilty of the two murders with which he is charged I direct you that as a matter of law you must find him guilty of capital murder.

'Members of the jury, on Sunday, June the thirteenth, Gwen Trent, aged eight, disappeared from her home in Eltham, Kent. She had been playing with friends in a small plot of waste land which lay at the end of the road in which she lived and just before four o'clock in the afternoon she told her playmates she was going home to tea. She did not arrive at her home, and her mother, who had made her promise to be back by four, went out to look for her. Her mother, in view of the terrible events over the past months in other parts of the country, had immediately become worried when her daughter was late.'

Defence counsel stood up. 'My Lord, it is with regret that I interrupt you, but I must protest at the reference to what has happened in other parts of the country.'

'Why so, Sir Patrick?'

'My Lord, I suggest the reason must be obvious.'

'Not sufficiently obvious for me to understand it, I fear. Perhaps you will make yourself clearer?'

'My Lord, the accused is charged with the murders of Gwen Trent and Charlotte Gains. To introduce irrelevant details such as your lordship has just done can only be to prejudice my client's case.'

'Sir Patrick, the jury can surely be presumed to know why the mother was so upset, so quickly? To hold otherwise is to credit them over the past twelve months with not having read a newspaper, listened to the wireless, or watched the television.'

'My Lord, since they can be presumed to know why she was so quickly upset there can be no excuse for unnecessarily and prejudicially underlining the fact.'

'Are you accusing me of prejudice towards the prisoner?'

'My Lord, should I do such a thing, your lordship would be the best judge of whether I were justified.' Defence counsel sat down.

The judge continued to address the jury.

'Members of the jury, the moment Mrs. Trent discovered that her daughter had left the piece of waste land, ten

6

minutes or a quarter of an hour before, she got in touch with the police and told them that her daughter was missing.

'The police immediately set in motion a nation-wide search for the missing girl, but tragically all their efforts were without success.

'On the twenty-fourth of September an anonymous letter was sent to the *Daily Express* in which the writer named the spot where the dead girl's body could be found. The police went to the indicated place, an overgrown ditch by the side of a minor road near the town of Hetcham, and discovered the body of Gwen Trent.

'Expert medical witnesses have testified that the unfortunate girl lived for about four days before she was finally murdered. During those four days she was barbarically tortured and most vilely assaulted. You have had, as I have, the most disagreeable duty of examining photographs of the dead girl's body and I venture to suggest there can be no doubt in any of your minds what terrible, unspeakable things she had to endure before she was finally granted the merciful release of death.

'Due to the interest, I am tempted to say perverted interest, any crime such as this one arouses in the minds of a certain section of the public, the police, in order to be able to carry on their work, had to screen off a large area around the point at which the body was found. It was from behind the canvas screen that they took the photographs of the onlookers about which you have heard so much.

'The chief superintendent told us very frankly that at this point little progress had been made by the police. He explained how difficult it is to solve a crime when it can be said that all the males in these islands over the age of puberty are potential suspects. There were no eye-witnesses

7

to see Gwen Trent led away by the unknown man and the police had been unable to uncover any trace of her movements from the moment she disappeared. It was for this reason, therefore, that they took a photograph of the watching crowd beyond the screens every fifteen minutes in the hope of identifying a man who spent an unusual length of time at the scene of this murder or who was present here and who had been present at the scene of the previous murder——'

'My Lord,' said defending counsel, as he stood up, 'this is too much.'

'Sir Patrick, I am not in the habit of suffering constant interruptions during my summing-up.'

'Equally, my Lord, it is not the habit for a judge to introduce into his summing-up prejudicial matters which lie wholly outside those at issue at the trial.'

'To what are you referring?'

'Your lordship well knows.'

'Did I know, Sir Patrick, I would not ask. You will either be more specific or remain silent.'

'My Lord, for the second time I must point out that the accused is charged with the murders of Gwen Trent and Charlotte Gains and with no other crime. It is prejudicial to him in the extreme to refer to other murders.'

'The jury are entitled to know how the identification from the photographs was made, since they have to make up their minds whether to accept the identification or not. To help them reach their decision on this point they must know the circumstances under which the previous photographs were taken.'

'My Lord, it is clear that if I am to have any chance of taking the point it will have to be before another court.'

'You have no right to speak like that, Sir Patrick.'

'On the contrary, my Lord, I suggest I have every right, both legally and morally.'

'You will sit down.'

'Very well, my Lord.' Counsel for the defence sat down.

The judge continued. 'Members of the jury, you have heard that frequently in crimes of this revolting nature the murderer returns to the place where he left the body because this affords him a monstrous satisfaction and gratification. The police had a set of photographs, taken two months previous, and they now compared those with the ones they took from behind the screens around the ditch where Gwen Trent's body had been found. The task was one of very great difficulty and complexity, but eventually, on the twenty-eighth of June, one man was recognized as having been present at both murder scenes. He was identified as George Krammer.

'It is yet another tragic feature of this case that the identification was only made on the day that Charlotte Gains disappeared. But I wish to make it quite clear that I am implying no criticism of the police. They did the best they could and no one could have done more.

'Charlotte Gains had gone to the shops with her brother, who was three years older. After buying some sweets they had an argument and as a consequence her brother left her to make her own way home. She never arrived back and when her brother returned on his own some time later Mrs. Gains immediately became extremely concerned. She notified the police and they alerted every force in the country.

'For four days the police were unable to make any progress. Late on the fourth day George Krammer was interviewed by the police in the village of Witham, on the main road between Bradham and Colchester. Chief Inspector Jones told you in evidence that Krammer denied any knowledge of the whereabouts of Charlotte Gains, but that there were some grains of sand visible on his trousers. An examination of his clothes was made and more sand was recovered. This sand, members of the jury, is of very great importance. It has a long and learned name, but for our purpose it is enough to remember that this sand is peculiar to one very small part of Essex and that no other deposit in the British Isles is known. This sand is found in an area of about three miles around Creemore. Krammer was asked whether he had been near here and he denied that he had. He said he had just come from Colchester and was driving directly to London and had not stopped anywhere before Witham. A search of the Creemore quarries was made and the body of Charlotte Gains was found. According to the medical evidence, she had only recently died, four days after she had disappeared. The cause of her death was the same as in the case of Gwen Trent. She had been tortured and most vilely assaulted. You have seen photographs of the dead girl . . .'

. . . . . .

At three-fifteen in the afternoon a shaft of sunlight coming in through the glass skylight of the courtroom covered Krammer. It seemed an outrageous thing to happen.

Krammer was so ordinary a person that it needed a distinct effort of will to forget the normal appearance and listen to the abnormal evidence. Before his arrest the papers had referred to the reign of terror by the unknown madman, but in the dock he seemed perfectly sane and far too insignificant to terrorize anyone.

At the age of thirty-eight, there was nothing about him to distinguish him from a thousand and one other men. He was five feet seven inches tall and weighed just over ten stone. He dressed neatly. His face was squarish, his chin sharp, his lips thin, and in repose his mouth suggested, if anything, a pleasant character. His eyes were light blue. He always kept his greying hair, receding at the temples, neatly brushed.

He was married, and had been for eight years, to a woman of no discernible character. She had no idea what her husband had been doing when he was away from home and the shock of finding out was so great that she suffered a serious mental breakdown. When she said she loved him she was telling the truth.

.   .   .   .   .

'Members of the jury, I am now going to remind you of the so-called verse the prisoner wrote when in custody. You will remember that defence counsel objected to the admissibility of this evidence, but in your absence I listened to arguments on this point and ruled that it was admissible. I quote:

> '"Look on the face of innocence,
> Conceive its purest thoughts,
> Look on the hands of innocence,
> The working claws of hell.
> The mind revolts, 'tis torn apart,
> And crucified to death.
> Desires they flame and multiply,
> They overwhelm and burn,
> Desires they torture, crucify,
> And murder them who know."

'I shall read to you certain of the cross-examination of the prisoner.

'Question: "Did you write this?" Prisoner: "Yes."

'Question: "Do you often write poetry?" Prisoner: "Sometimes."

'Question: "Is it all like this?" Prisoner: "I don't know. I tear it up."

'Question: "Would you agree that this is a very odd kind of verse?" Prisoner: "No."

'Question: "Don't you think most people would refer to the hands of innocence in complimentary terms?" Prisoner: "I don't know."

'Question: "Why are the hands of innocence the working claws of hell?" Prisoner: "That's just poetic licence."

'Question: "Is it because of what those hands have done?" Prisoner: "No."

'Question: "Do you call them the working claws of hell because of the hellish things they have done to Gwen Trent and Charlotte Gains?" Prisoner: "No. No. I tell you, it's poetic licence. It doesn't mean anything. It's nothing to do with me."

'Question: "Isn't it? You wrote, 'The mind revolts, 'tis torn apart, And crucified to death.' From what does the mind revolt?" Prisoner: "The poem doesn't say."

'Question: "I suggest that, in fact, it most certainly does say. The mind revolts from the most terribly misnamed hands of innocence. Whose mind revolts from them?" Prisoner: "No one's."

'Question: " 'Desires they flame and multiply, They overwhelm and burn'. What kind of desires are those?" Prisoner: "I don't know."

'Question: "But you wrote the poem?" Prisoner. "You don't have to know the meaning of everything you write."

'Question: "Would you agree that these desires must be terrible in character?" Prisoner: "I don't know."

'Question: "But it's a very nasty list, isn't it? These

desires are said to overwhelm, burn, torture, crucify, and murder." Prisoner: "That's only a way of talking."

'Question: "I put it to you that this poem accurately describes the appalling state of your mind?" Prisoner: "No, it's nothing to do with me."

'Members of the jury, you may well feel, as the counsel for the prosecution vigorously maintained, there cannot be much doubt about the true meaning of this poem.'

Counsel for the defence rose and spoke wearily. 'My Lord, the jury really must be left to make their own decisions.'

'I quite agree, Sir Patrick.'

'From the way your lordship spoke they might well have felt they were receiving a directive.'

'I hardly think they are that stupid, Sir Patrick.'

Counsel for the defence sat down, turned, and spoke to his junior. 'The bastard,' he said.

.   .   .   .   .   .

When the jury returned and were asked for their verdict there was silence in the courtroom. It was a moment of drama, even though no one had the slightest doubt about what the verdict would be.

'Guilty,' said the foreman of the jury, who looked like a prosperous butcher.

People coughed, sighed, shuffled their feet, and whispered to each other.

Krammer suddenly began to shout. 'I couldn't stop myself. I had to do it. And if I hadn't done it you couldn't have proved yourselves by trying me. You wanted me to do it, so that all of you could find someone to spit on.'

'Be silent,' ordered the judge, his long, hard, unemotional face looking under the slate-coloured wig like some cold carving of justice incarnate. 'George Krammer, you have very rightly been found guilty of the capital murder of Gwen

13

Trent and Charlotte Gains. It is the sentence of this court that you shall suffer death in the manner authorized by law.'

.　　　.　　　.　　　.　　　.

The death sentence was commuted by the Home Secretary to one of imprisonment for life because of the forthcoming Bill to abolish capital punishment.

Two

Lettworth Prison had been built in 1885. It was a disgrace to any country, more especially to one which prided itself on believing in the inherent humanity of man. The whole place stank of misery, defeat, and abandonment. It housed one thousand two hundred and thirty-two prisoners instead of the five hundred it was designed for, and most men were three to a cell. Fifteen-foot-high walls surrounded it, and inside, at the geographical centre, was the round tower from which ran the five wings, like the spokes of a wheel. In the round tower the warders could, by walking only a few yards, look down each wing in turn and make certain all was in order. Along the inside of the fifteen-foot walls were the workshops, laundry, recreation huts, greenhouses, and administration block. Immediately outside the walls were the staff quarters, almost as bleak-looking as the prison. If the prison enslaved the prisoners it also enslaved the warders: if it dehumanized the prisoners it dehumanized the warders.

As in every prison, class distinctions were as important inside as outside. The aristocracy included petermen and screwsmen, the middle class included droppers and drummers, the working class included creeps and hoisters. The outcasts, the untouchables, were the sex-offenders.

There was no honour among thieves: only a bitter determination to steal anything that was worth stealing, to lie whenever possible, and to keep silent at all other times.

The trusties were despised and the leaders were hated. The snout barons were the uncrowned rulers. Rehabilitation was a word that the prisoners laughed at and the warders detested. The warders knew that because the prisoners were bad they were good: therefore, at every reform which lessened the burden on the prisoners and so made them less bad, the warders felt themselves to have been made less good. Warders and prisoners united in only one thing: hatred of the sex men.

There were brown-hatters, palones, poufs, or queers: whichever name was preferred. And there was Krammer.

Krammer was in cell No. A5, which was on the top floor of the wing nearest to the huge outside gates. The other two men in the cell were Younger and Martineu. Younger was the most powerful snout baron and Martineu was one of his runners: Martineu, a half-caste from Barbados, was handy with the knife he had made from a chisel stolen from one of the workshops. Younger did everything in his power to make certain Krammer's life was hell. Younger had two daughters, maybe more, and although he had not seen them in fourteen years he said that he thought about them every time he looked at Krammer.

After he had been in prison some months, Krammer was beaten up. He complained. The assistant governor who heard the complaint had a daughter of nine. He asked Krammer whether he expected a life that was all roses. Krammer was beaten up again for having complained. Everything stealable was stolen from him, he was threatened with being murdered, and he had to live twenty-four hours of the day with the terrifying knowledge that there was not one man in the prison, except the chaplain, who was ready to offer him anything but hate.

In his utter despair he tried to strangle himself during the night, but the effort was a farcically inefficient one which

16

made Younger laugh: in any case, he was never going to be allowed to escape that easily. He went to the chaplain, seeking the comfort of religion, but gained only that man's sympathy.

So he decided to escape. On the face of it, it was as ridiculous as his attempt to commit suicide. A prison escape called for a toughness of character and body such as he certainly did not possess: but he had something even more useful, an utter desperation. He also had the one job in prison which allowed an unorganized escape to be possible. He worked in the greenhouses and these were near the administration block. Some of the warders worked there and from time to time they seemed to forget they were still within prison confines and when it was really hot they removed their jackets and caps and hung them up somewhere handy.

It was July. The weather was hot and, apart from some torrential thunderstorms, fine. This made the prisoners restless. It reminded them of the outside world beyond the fifteen-foot wall which was topped with inward-curving metal spikes that had gone rusty. There was a fight in the workshops which immediately turned into a general brawl. A warder was injured before the fight was subdued. The men concerned were taken before the governor and they received fourteen days in the punishment cells on restricted diet and loss of remission. Martineu—due to deal with another prisoner who seemed to be challenging Younger's position—was one of those men, and that night, in their cell, Younger blamed Krammer for everything that had gone wrong and hit him twice in the face and once in the guts and laughed like hell when Krammer tried to be sick but failed. A warder heard the noise and looked through the spyhole to see what the trouble was. When he saw

Krammer, doubled up on the cell floor, struggling to over-come the spasms of nausea, he walked away.

Lights, except for the all-night ones, went out at 9 p.m., and even though it was still daylight outside, the slits in the cells reduced this to no more than a glimmer. Krammer dragged himself up into his bunk and gradually the pain and the nausea receded. His mind recorded only complete and utter despair for a long time, but then it gradually became fixed on the knowledge that tomorrow he would escape. Eventually he slept. He dreamt of the tarns and mountains of Cumberland amongst which he had been born.

When he awoke it was 6 a.m. He lay in the bunk, terrified by the knowledge of what he was going to do and what would happen to him if he failed.

The bells rang at 6.30. He got up and washed in cold water. Younger lay in the bunk until the last possible moment, jeering at him and threatening him with every possible form of vileness. He tried not to listen as he made his bunk, exactly to regulations, even though Younger would rip it apart before inspection time.

Cell doors were opened for the emptying of slops. He went along the passage to the lavatories and used the one with a painted red cross on the door. It was for prisoners suffering from V.D. Just one more bitter humiliation he was made to undergo.

The prisoners lined up outside the cells and filed down the metal stairs to the mess-hall for breakfast. They served themselves, cafeteria-style, and then sat down at the plain wooden tables. Krammer had his four thick slices of bread and pat of margarine stolen by a man who was doing ten years for G.B.H. A watching warder saw the incident and ignored it.

After breakfast they returned to their cells to clean them.

18

Krammer did all the work and Younger made the job three times as difficult as it should have been. A warder came round to check if any prisoners wanted to book to see the governor, the doctor, or the chaplain. After that the prisoners went down and out into the yard, where they split up into work parties for the carpenter's shop, tailor's shop, cobbler's shop, general workroom, laundry, gardens, or the greenhouses. After the end of the work period, and before lunch, there was the exercise period. Between each wing of the prison were concentric circles of concrete around which the prisoners had to walk for half an hour. Those going round one circle moved in the opposite direction to those in the next: from a distance it looked like some form of P.T. display.

At lunch Krammer's meat was stolen from his plate as he turned to answer a question. He did not bother even to try to see who had taken it, but just stolidly ate the potatoes and tasteless, watery cabbage. After lunch he returned to the greenhouses and half an hour later told the gardener instructor, not a uniformed officer, that he had to go and see the chief officer. There was a warder who should have accompanied him, but the warder was hot and tired and damned if he was going to put himself out for that bastard Krammer. So Krammer was allowed to go on his own across the concreted yard to the administration block.

So many things could, and should, have combined to render his escape attempt a ridiculous failure. But the heat had made everyone lethargic and also had made many warders remove their coats and hats.

He went into the administration block by the side door and found a warder's hat and coat hanging up just inside. He put them on and waited in the small lavatory after locking the door. He could see the main gates by lowering the top sash window a few inches.

At four o'clock the relief warders entered the prison. When the last man was inside, the small door to the left of the huge gates was locked. Then, a quarter of an hour later, it was unlocked to allow those warders now off duty to go out. As they went, they gave their names to the two men guarding the door.

Krammer, so terrified he almost could not move, left the lavatory and the administration block and walked across the yard. The nearer warder on gate duty grumpily asked him what in the name of hell had been holding him up and did he think no one else had anything to do but open and shut the bloody door all day? Krammer mumbled an answer and gave a name. The door was opened and he went out into the road. The door was slammed shut behind him and he heard the bolts sliding home. He stood in the sunshine, blinking nervously, wondering what he was going to do and where he was going to go. A double-decker bus, painted red and cream, went by and without really thinking about what he was doing, he felt the breast pocket of the coat he was now wearing. There was a wallet inside and when he opened it he found it contained four one-pound notes and one ten-shilling note. The fates really couldn't have been kinder to him.

. . . . .

The inspector, sitting behind his desk, finally dozed off and immediately was transported away from the hot, stuffy room at the police station to a beach somewhere in Arcadia.

A bluebottle buzzed round the room, saw the inspector's bald head, and settled on it. The bluebottle seemed also to be about to fall asleep.

The telephone rang. The inspector awoke with a start and the bluebottle took off, buzzing loudly. The inspector lifted the receiver. 'Yes?'

'Krammer's escaped. Alert all sections J.A.P.'

The inspector no longer felt sleepy.

Three

For years it had been obvious to those people who could think without prejudice about such matters that more and more of the police forces in England, Scotland, and Wales would have to be amalgamated, even if the ultimate answer to the growing efficiency and mobility of criminals, a national force, was politically unacceptable. J.A.P., the first tentative move to break down the geographical barriers of borough or county, and the psychological barriers of localized chauvinism, was handicapped by many things, among them the cumbersome command with six chief constables and six Standing Joint Committees trying to agree policy, the traditional rivalry between forces, and the sheer novelty of the occasion.

Harper, one of the six chief constables concerned in this experiment, had typified the more hidebound spirit. An excellent administrator, he lacked the ability to see beyond the rules and regulations and could not appreciate the need to forgo his blind jealousy for his command. In the end, however, he had been persuaded to agree to recommending to his Standing Joint Committee that Joint Area, Policing (J.A.P.) be adopted. Three days later, back at his H.Q., he had called into his room the deputy chief constable and the two assistant chief constables. He told them what had happened and added that as the whole idea was obviously a bloody silly waste of time it wasn't worth losing a good officer to it. Agar could be posted to Section 1.

Agar was the least happy of the section commanders of J.A.P. It had been made quite clear to him that he had only been appointed because his chief constable had no faith in the idea. Experience soon showed that since the kind of crime for which J.A.P. had come into being was, by its nature, a relatively rare occurrence, much of Agar's time had to be spent on other matters and he became a kind of odd-job man, without any of the sense of pride and purpose that came from running a divisional C.I.D.

He was a well-built, broad-shouldered man of forty-three with fixed—some said blindly biased—views on certain things. Like the greater proportion of serving police officers, he was certain that punishment had to be retributive as well as a deterrent. He believed in the *Lex talionis*: the Old Testament cry of eye for eye, tooth for tooth.

His personnel report at H.Q. contained the fatal entry in red that meant he could forget all about ambition.

Form 4/SP.

RESTRICTED. (Chief Constable, Deputy Chief Constable, Assistant Chief Constables, Chief Super., Admin.)

AGAR, William Boyce. 43. Married, Caroline (*Née* Barranty). 1 Son.

H.M. Forces 1940–1945. 1st Lieut., Eastern Counties Light Infantry. Mentioned in Dispatches, Twice.

County Police Force (H Division) 1946. 2 years Probation. Confirmed P.C. 1948. 2 Letters of Commendation, Divisional Superintendent. T27 Reports, Excellent.

6 months C.I.D. aide. Approved. C.I.D. 1950 (M Division). Letter of Commendation, D.D.I.

Highest marks of year, county qualifying exams. Sergeant.

Detective Sergeant (P Division) 1952.

Commendation bravery, Allworth Magistrates' Court, 1953.
Chief Constable's Commendation and Lord Bourne Medal.

Challon House, 1953. Honours, final exam.
Detective Inspector (Q Division) 1958. T28 Reports, Excellent.
Best Divisional Crime Figures (53%). 3 Letters of Commendation,
Detective Superintendent (H.Q.)

Detective Chief Inspector (H.Q.) 1963.

*1964. Guilty, 3rd degree violence, prisoner. Sentence of dismissal
force reduced on appeal. Demotion, D.I., loss of 3 years' pension
rights.*

Detective Inspector (R Division) 1964.

Transferred Joint Area, Policing 1964.

Caroline (*née* Barranty). Preyton Grammar School. Matriculated.
Secretarial. Socially, group 1.

He had not denied the violence at the police hearing and,
typically, he was not even going to try to defend himself
on that point, but eventually it had all come out in evidence.
The teen-age thugs had robbed the old woman of twenty-
three pounds and half killed her in doing so. Some pains-
taking work on his part had uncovered their identity. They
had shown no remorse whatsoever at what they had done
to her and were completely indifferent about the injuries
she had suffered. When he had arrested them the elder of
the two had jeered at him and prophesied (correctly) that
the courts would be soft enough to put him and his pal
on probation, which would make the twenty-three quid
very easy money. Agar had hit the youth so hard that he
suffered a broken nose when he twisted round and fell on
the corner of a chair. Agar's mother was the same age as
that old woman.

He appealed against dismissal from the force and his
appeal was partially successful. But his police career was

24

ruined. Where before he had had every chance of reaching the rank of assistant chief constable, or higher, now he would be retired a D.I. . . . . Always provided, that was, he did not lose his temper again and beat-up some pimply, sweating, long-haired slob who thought the law was so soft it paid to hurt the weak and the old.

After that hearing he had been posted to R Division, which covered the slum areas on the north-east coast where violence was a nightly occurrence and the crime-rate graph climbed steadily upwards. Then, following the Krammer case and the formation of J.A.P., he was banished to the command of Section 1, where it seemed to him that he must either stagnate mentally from boredom or reach breaking-point from a sense of frustration. But then Krammer escaped from Lettworth jail.

* * * * *

He was in his room at H.Q. when there was a call to go to the chief superintendent's (Admin.) office.

Parkinson was fat and in the hot weather he perspired continuously, as if he had sprung a leak. Standing by the side of his desk was one of the two assistant chief constables.

' 'Afternoon, sir,' said Agar.

Parkinson spoke rapidly, his words slurred because of his ill-fitting false teeth. 'Have you heard?'

'What?'

'Krammer's out.'

'Out?'

'Escaped,' snapped the assistant chief constable. 'The silly bastards just let him walk straight out of the gates about three-quarters of an hour ago.'

Agar stared at the fat, perspiring chief superintendent

25

as he tried to adjust his mind to the knowledge that Krammer was free.

Parkinson spoke. 'J.A.P.'s been alerted. I want you to drive up to the prison and try to find out what you can that will help us land him if he comes this way.'

'What's he wearing, sir? Prison outfit?'

'He pinched a warder's jacket and hat. On top of everything else, they say there was about five quid in the wallet.'

'Is there any hint about which way he's gone?'

'None. As soon as the public gets the news and start looking for him we should land him.' The chief superintendent gave some carefully detailed orders which were designed to show the A.C.C. how on the ball he was, then he dismissed Agar. Agar returned to his room, which he shared with one of the D.I.s on the H.Q. staff. As he stacked up the papers he had been working on the other man, Clanton, walked in.

'Krammer's escaped,' said Agar.

'My God!' Clanton's face expressed the sense of shock he felt. He picked up a pencil and fidgeted with it. 'If he isn't grabbed quickly he might get hold of another girl——'

'Why not?' cut in Agar harshly. 'He's got the maximum punishment already. Half a dozen more girls can't add anything to that. Look, Jack, I'm supposed to be dealing with this report for Alec—tell him what's happened when he starts belly-aching for it.'

'Sure. Which way's Krammer heading?'

'No one knows.'

'Probably he'll make for his wife.'

'Not him. He's enough brain to know that if he does that he'll be back behind bars before he's time enough to know he's really free.'

'Depends what you mean by brains.'

'Got any fags? I've run right out.'

'Here are five.' He took them out of a packet of twenty and handed them across. 'I hope to God someone grabs him quickly before he has time to do anything.'

Agar did not bother to answer, but left the room in a rush and went along the passage to the main staircase and down to the ground floor. His car, a rather battered Morris 1000, was parked at the rear of the building, between two dog-handlers' vans. He backed it, turned, and drove on to the road.

His house was on the north-west side of Carriford and because of the traffic it took him fifteen frustrating minutes to reach it. He left the car in the road and went into the house. Caroline, his wife, was in the kitchen, cooking.

'I've got to go to Lettworth,' he said.

'Not now, surely, Bill?'

' 'Fraid so.'

'But what about your meal? It can be ready in only half an hour.'

'It'll have to be a sandwich, or something, to see me through until the other end. Krammer's broken loose.'

She reached up with her right hand and touched her cheek with her fingers. 'Oh, no! Oh, my God!' She was not a beautiful woman, but she had an inner sereneness which made her attractive. She was inclined to be plump, but fairly rigid dieting kept that plumpness in check. When Agar had ruined his police career by hitting that young, jeering thug it was she who had forced him to accept the consequences calmly and not to resign from the force after his dismissal was quashed and he was demoted.

Agar lit one of the cigarettes he had borrowed from Clanton. 'He escaped in warder's clothes and has something like five quid in cash.' He looked at his watch. 'That was a little over an hour ago, so now he's probably thirty or forty miles from the prison.'

'But what can you do at Lettworth?'

'Make myself really unpopular. The local lads will have taken the place apart, trying to find out something, and then I'll come busting along and go through the whole thing again.'

'Bill, what are the odds of catching him before he . . . before anything happens?'

He tried to speak with far more certainty than he felt. 'There's not really any fear of that. Pretty soon the whole country will know he's loose. All TV programmes have been asked to put out his photograph at regular intervals and it's hoped to get a last edition of the evening papers out with the news and photos. The wireless will issue warnings.'

'Even so . . .'

'He's on the run, Carry, and won't have time for worrying about anything but keeping free. When a man's like that he begins to panic because he knows the whole world's against him and that does something to his mind so that he starts seeing and hearing things which don't exist.' He watched her begin to make some sardine sandwiches and then he hurried upstairs to change into a clean shirt. The journey ahead of him was just over seventy miles and he hoped like hell that when he reached the end of it he would be told that Krammer had been recaptured.

Four

Stoneyacre stood on the misnamed Cambrian Plateau,
thirty-nine miles from the coastal town of Raleton. Its
name dated from the Middle Ages when farmers had to
accept the soil as they found it. Even in present times the
ground for some distance needed an abnormal amount
of dung or fertilizer to keep it in good heart. As with so
many places close to London, the planners and builders
had not hesitated to rape the countryside and the charm
the village had once possessed was destroyed for ever by
the waves of concrete and bricks. Few people seemed to
care about this.

Charles Bramswell, at forty-four, was a man with a chip
on his shoulder the size of an oak tree. He knew himself to
be a failure and tried to conceal this fact by behaving as
someone who was too great a radical for the world into
which he had been born. He had married in 1944, when
still in uniform and with money to burn. Betty Bramswell,
his wife, had taken too long to realize that when he was out
of uniform and living at home there would cease to be
money for burning. She blamed him for what she called
their 'poverty'. When their neighbours, scrap-dealers, drove
past in a new Rover 2000 she would remember their second-
hand mini-van and would suffer a sensation that was akin
to physical pain. Although not as violently radical as her
husband, she had no time for a world which rewarded
scrap-dealers so much more highly than schoolteachers:

being essentially more sensible than her husband, she sometimes wondered why he had never tried to deal in scrap.

Their daughter Sarah was surprisingly gay in view of the rows which so often went on at home. At the age of twelve she had managed to discover how to accept her parents with all their obvious faults and yet love them. She had also learned to laugh at them. When, some time before, her father, who had been met by almost total apathy when he tried to form a local C.N.D. branch, led four members on a route march to the war memorial on the anniversary of Hiroshima she was the loudest of the jeering schoolchildren: however, being intelligent, she stood to the back of the group. She gave promise of becoming beautiful, with a face a little off centre so that the halves did not exactly match: there would be great character in her face, character she had inherited from her parents who had never been able properly to use their share of it.

Bramswell taught modern languages at Carriford Grammar School (founded by Henry VIII and granted the motto 'Honour thy Mistress, Learning' just after Henry VIII had honoured his one-time mistress and later queen, Anne Boleyn, by beheading her). Had he obtained a degree, his salary might have been one he could have considered almost adequate, but when he gained a scholarship to Cambridge before the war his parents had not had enough money to be able to support him there and when he could have gone after the war, under the ex-servicemen's scheme, he was too busy enjoying himself with Betty.

He looked up from the pile of exercise books before him and stared at the far wall and the crumbling plaster. He was reminded of the slates which were missing from the roof and the chimney-stack which needed re-pointing. All he needed was just a little money, he thought with bitter sarcasm.

Betty came into the room and sat down in one of the worn chairs. She flapped the front of her dress against herself. 'It's so damned hot I'm being basted in my own juices. We've got to have a fridge.'

'What's wrong with those earthenware pots? If you keep them damp——'

'In this sort of heat? Come off it. In any case, I haven't time to muck around like that.'

'We can't afford a fridge.'

'Surely we could just stretch to one of the very cheap ones?'

He shook his head.

'Then what about asking for that raise from the headmaster, or whoever it is you go to for money? Say we're living in a slum and could you have something that just begins to smell of a living wage. It says in the paper that the men on the new motorway are making over forty quid a week.'

'We've been promised a salary review.'

'Promises never fed anyone.'

'I can't do more. I'm not one of the property bastards who can make another fortune just by signing a contract.'

'I wouldn't mind being a bastard if I was a property one,' she said, and suddenly grinned. 'I'd even sign away Buck House if you paid me enough.'

He smiled back at her. Often the bitterness of their lives prevented them from standing aside and laughing at themselves, but occasionally it did not.

He opened a packet of cigarettes and threw one across to her. 'I had a word with George today. He says the capital gains tax is to be increased immediately until it really hurts.'

She shrugged her shoulders. Her immediate need for a refrigerator was far greater than her interest in capital gains tax. She agreed with much of her husband's political philosophy, but could never become so concerned about matters as he did. She had been astonished when he had organized the C.N.D. march, because it had been obvious from the beginning that it could only arouse derision and he was a man who normally could not bear the thought that he might be made to look a fool. It often angered her that a man who cared so much about so many things in the world should apparently care so little about the life he actually led that he would not fight to better it.

'What's the time?' he asked, breaking into her thoughts.

'Nearly five to six.'

'Then we'll get the news on the telly.' He stood up and crossed to the television set and switched on ITV. Only rarely did he watch B.B.C.: they were part of the Establishment.

The advertisements ceased and the news began after a time check. The announcer said that Krammer had escaped from Lettworth jail that afternoon. He was wearing a warder's hat and jacket and a prisoner's dark blue trousers. There was no reason to suppose there was any danger to the public, but everyone was asked to be on the look-out for him and if they saw him to report that fact to the nearest police station. A photograph of Krammer was shown. The announcer went on to say why Krammer had been in jail, as if there were viewers who might already have forgotten.

'That's terrible,' said Betty, in a high voice.

'They'll soon catch him,' he replied indifferently. 'Shut up and let's listen about the tax.'

'But suppose they don't. Look what he did to those poor kids. . . .'

Krammer's picture disappeared and the news continued. To Bramswell's openly expressed disgust there was nothing about the increase in capital gains tax.

'It's terrible,' said Betty, as the news ended.

'You're dead right there. How could George——'

'I'm talking about Krammer,' she snapped.

'The police'll land him soon enough. I must get on with these bloody papers. Thirty-nine boys and not one of 'em has yet learned even the rudiments of French grammar.'

She switched off the set. 'It's odd, Charles, how you're so good at languages.'

He picked up a pencil and crossed out something on the right-hand page of the top exercise book. 'Some people can write, some can paint: I can speak languages and sweet Fanny Hill good it does me.'

'I know. But why doesn't it do you any good?'

'You know as well as I do. My parents couldn't afford to support me to take up that scholarship to Queens' College. Those were the days when no one wanted hoi polloi educated in case they got ideas above their station. That's why I haven't got a degree and that's why no one pays me for being brilliant.'

The door opened, and Sarah their daughter came in. As usual, she looked as though she had been blown all the way by the wind. She was tall for her age and her figure was developing fast. She had merry eyes, a snub nose, a mouth which was usually grinning, and blonde hair almost always in disarray. 'Gwen's asked me to her party,' she said excitedly.

'Who's Gwen?' queried her mother.

'Gwen Bailey. You know, the girl with the sticking-out teeth in front which make her look like a donkey. Her father owns the garage and is fab wealthy. She's got more records at home than Jacko has in his shop.' Sarah went across to the table and tried to push past her father. 'Move over, Dad, I want a piece of cake.' Receptive to the atmosphere, she correctly guessed that her parents were on reasonably amicable terms.

'You're always gorging yourself,' he said, as he moved to let her past.

'Gerty says I've got worms.'

'Don't be disgusting,' said her mother.

'Are they disgusting?' Sarah cut herself a large slice of the home-made sponge cake. 'It's all right for the party, isn't it, Mum?'

'When is it?'

'Tomorrow evening. Gwen said the Farm House Trio are going to be there, but that would be just too fant for words. I'd swoon twice. Gwen says that what with all the restrictions, or something, her dad will make a fortune now. She said he made all his money after the war selling things he wasn't supposed to. Is that right?'

'I expect so,' answered her father.

'What time does the party start?' asked Betty, as she drew on the cigarette for the last time and then threw the stub into the fireplace.

'It starts at seven and everyone's got to be there then.'

'And when's it finish? Nine?'

'You're so with the dinosaurs, Mum. It doesn't finish until eleven. It's real. I told you, there's dancing and——'

'Then you can't go.'

Sarah had been about to eat a piece of cake and she now held it in front of her mouth. She stared at her mother with open disbelief. 'Can't go?'

'You're not coming home on your own after dark.'

'But it's only ten minutes——'

'You're not walking back and that's that.'

Sarah knew from her mother's tone of voice that her decision was final. She slowly ate the mouthful of cake. She reflected that her parents were always doing real nutty things, but this was plain cruel. 'Why not? I've walked before.'

'There's a reason.' Betty hesitated, but quickly decided to tell the truth. 'That very nasty man, Krammer, has escaped from jail.'

'But what's he got to do with Gwen's party?'

'Until he's safely back in jail, you're not walking anywhere at night-time.'

'Dad can fetch me in the van, can't he?'

'He's going to a meeting.'

'One of his stupid old meetings?'

'That's quite enough from you.'

'But, Mum, Allyson's going and her father's bringing her back in their car. They could bring me back, couldn't they?'

Betty hesitated, because she knew what this party meant to Sarah.

'Please, Mum, please.'

'Very well, but only if Allyson's father agrees to bring you all the way back to this house.'

Sarah ate the rest of the cake. After a bit she asked: 'What did that man do to the girls, Mum? You never really explained.'

'Something very nasty and that's all you need know about it.' Betty Bramswell refused to say anything more. For one who prided herself on being liberally minded to a degree, there was a strangely puritanical and prudish streak to her character and she was not going to discuss with her daughter anything so filthy as the details of the Krammer case.

'But, Mum——'

'How about some silence for me to get on with my work?' snapped Bramswell.

'*Parlez-vous français?*' asked Sarah pertly.

35

Five

Agar drove straight to Lettworth Prison. He spoke to one of the assistant governors and the chief officer and, as expected, learned nothing. He then asked if he could interview one or both of Krammer's cell-mates and was told that that was quite unnecessary. Krammer was hated so much, a hatred increased because of his successful jail-break, that any prisoner who could have helped authority would already have done so. However, by use of a great deal of tact, Agar finally secured the permission he sought.

Ten minutes later Younger was brought to one of the interview rooms on the ground floor of E block. He acted in his usual surly and belligerent manner, but he was ready to talk. Krammer was gallows-meat and if he, Younger, knew so much as a bleeding whisper he'd pass it on, even to a bleeding split.

After giving Younger a couple of cigarettes, which was sending coals to Newcastle, and listening for a few minutes to the monotonous stream of obscenity with which Younger described Krammer, Agar stood up. 'Will you let someone hear if you get to know anything?'

'I'll shout it from the bleeding roof-tops, mate, don't worry none on that score.'

'Is it worth talking to anyone else?'

'No. There ain't anyone in the place what had anything to do with that bleeder. Excepting the dog-collar, but he'd do anything for a convert.'

'Thanks for the chat.'

'Been a pleasure, mate.' Younger swaggered out of the room, winking at the warder who stepped out from the wall and walked behind him.

Agar left the interview room and returned to the assistant governor's office, where he asked for the home address of the prison chaplain. He then left the prison and as the small door was slammed shut behind him he involuntarily shivered: that was one of the most ominous sounds in the world.

He sat in his car and wondered what to do. If he saw the chaplain now he would be too late, by the time he reached his hotel, to be served a meal, and he was very hungry: yet if he returned for a meal it would be too late afterwards to visit the chaplain. He reluctantly decided he must follow the dictates of duty, not his stomach.

The chaplain's house, within half a mile of the prison, was one of a row of depressed, rather shabby, buildings. Smith, the chaplain, was a thin, elderly man, who was wearing sports coat and grey flannel trousers. They went into the sitting-room and Agar saw the tray, by the side of one of the well-worn armchairs, on which was the other's supper. He tried not to look too hard at the meal, which had only just been started, but clearly he had made his own hunger rather obvious.

'May I offer you something to eat?'

'No, thanks. When I get back to the hotel——'

'You're too late for that now. Our hotels keep very strict catering hours, as I once discovered to my cost when my bishop was visiting me. I'll get you something. I live on my own, so that housekeeping merely consists of opening tins. All I have to do is open one more for you. But maybe you'd like a little sherry first?'

Before long Agar was thoroughly enjoying tinned salmon, lettuce salad, cheese and biscuits.

'You're wanting to know if I can help you over Krammer?' said Smith, after they had both finished eating.

'Yes.'

'Have I any idea where he's gone and, if so, will I tell you?'

'One of the prisoners told me you saw quite a lot of him?'

'He was one of the few men in the prison—sometimes I would be tempted to say the only one—who genuinely and desperately wanted my help.' Smith sighed. 'I couldn't really help him, though: perhaps no mere human could.'

'Probably not,' said Agar harshly.

Smith took off his spectacles and polished them with a handkerchief. 'He was the most mentally tortured and unhappy man I have ever met. The other prisoners persecuted him without mercy and the warders connived at this persecution. I remonstrated about this with the governor, but although he's a very sincere man, he has certain . . . I shall call them blind spots.'

'Most of us have blind spots when it comes to dealing with a man who's done what he has.'

'Is it, then, so easy, Inspector?'

'Is what easy?'

'To judge. You see, I learned enough about him to be quite certain that he acted from a compulsion in which there was absolutely no use of will. He didn't *decide* to attack a girl: this terrible thing was far stronger than that. Most criminals decide to commit a crime, which means they've used the God-given force of free will and come to an evil decision: but Krammer was never given that chance. So is his crime worse than that of the man who deliberately chooses the path of evil: surely mental sickness negates any moral responsibility?'

38

'The court found him sane.'

'Forgive me, Inspector, but we both know that the findings of a court in this respect are neither accurate nor unbiased. Courts do not recognize compulsion, but any enlightened man of medicine will tell you such a thing exists. I'm only too aware of the fact that the results of his crime were infinitely worse than those of an ordinary criminal, but surely we dare not judge criminals by results? If so, the criminal who is unsuccessful is less of a criminal than the one who is successful.'

'A man like him is so rotten there's only one way of dealing with him.'

'You obviously won't expect me to begin to agree. Krammer spoke to me of the terrible inner struggles he had had: he described his mind as having been split into two. One half would want to commit some ghastly crime while the other half would be appalled by this unspeakable desire. Inspector, arrest and conviction was what Krammer desperately needed because these two things made him suffer for what he had done and in such suffering he expected to find release from his terrible compulsion. Only his fellow prisoners could not show him any Christian spirit and they made his suffering too great. No man is an island, Inspector, entire of itself. No man can do without any hand of friendship.'

Agar stubbed out his cigarette. 'Are you telling me he's changed?'

'Yes. I believe he is a soul who was lost in the blackest reaches of hell but who began to climb out of them when he was punished by the society he had outraged. I believe that, right now, he is struggling to find himself as a man might try to find himself after travelling for a lifetime through a tunnel and who suddenly comes to the end and open countryside. It is because of this miracle of rebirth

39

that I thank God he was spared from execution and so lived to escape.'

'And in your philosophy did all those girls have to be tortured to death in order for him to find himself?'

'I wish to God I knew the answer,' said Smith quietly. 'I just wish to God I knew.'

Fifteen minutes later Agar left the house and drove into the centre of the town. He parked his car in the hotel car park, booked in, and collected his key from the sleepy night porter, and made his way up to his room.

He lowered the window so that the light breeze could try to dispel some of the stifling heat. He undressed and put on the pair of pyjamas which Caroline always said made him look like a Chinese mandarin, climbed into bed, and lit a last cigarette after telling himself he wouldn't. He thought about their son, reading law, and then about the chaplain. Had he been talking a lot of religious nonsense? Could anyone really say that the man who wilfully stole a loaf of bread was a worse criminal than the man who unwilfully tortured girls to death? And yet how could a man resist an irresistible compulsion? He, Agar, reckoned himself to be an ordinary, decent man. Yet suppose some compulsion seized him. Did that turn him into something unutterably foul when there was absolutely nothing he could do to stop himself acting as he did?

This led him to wonder if it really could be true that the escaped Krammer was no longer a threat to any girl he met. Was he hiding somewhere, grappling with himself, perhaps even winning the battle?

As Agar turned off the light, after stubbing out the cigarette, he suddenly realized that this was the first time he had ever thought of Krammer as a human being.

With daybreak, the hunt for Krammer gained momentum, and although it certainly was not impossible he had gone more than a hundred miles, this was the area of maximum strength search. The area covered all the Home Counties. For once, almost every criminal known to the police was ready to grass, but not one of them had any worthwhile information to give. Krammer's house was under constant watch, but the pathetic Mrs. Krammer, shunned by everyone even though she was innocent of anything, remained alone.

By 9 a.m., reports from the public had swollen to such a flood that they threatened to swamp the staff who were available to deal with them. Krammer was seen in a hundred and seventy-five cities and towns and twenty-four men were wrongly taken into custody by their fellow citizens. The watch on all airports and ports was maintained at maximum security, although no one believed he would try to go abroad.

The incipient hysteria, which gripped so many people, never really got out of hand because of the restrained and high standard of reporting of the radio, TV, and Press. However, in some cases this hysteria did take an active form: fifteen women reported they had been attacked and raped by Krammer and in not one case had anything at all happened to them. Fifty-three girls did not turn up at their respective schools and when informed of this their respective parents were certain the worst had happened until it was discovered that each one of the fifty-three had decided that here was a golden chance to play truant for the day.

At 11.30 a householder in the stockbroker area of Surrey reported that his potting shed, at the end of the large garden, had been broken into during the night and that it looked as if someone had slept there. Detectives went to the house and conducted an intensive search of the garden and the shed. They found a projecting nail in one of the shed's uprights on which was a thread of blue serge. It could have come from the coat Krammer was wearing, but equally on such scanty evidence it could have come from the coat of some tramp. But wouldn't a layabout tramp have stolen some of the many small and portable items around? It was assumed for the moment that Krammer had spent the night in this shed. The search became centralized about this area. Detectives and uniformed policemen toured the streets in cars, went into public houses, schools, shops, and cinemas, and asked for help and gave advice.

   .   .   .   .   .

At H.Q., Carriford, Agar went up the one floor to his room after reporting to Chief Superintendent Parkinson. Clanton was out and he had the place to himself. He rang up Caroline to tell her he was safely back from Lettworth and then he sat down behind his desk and stared at the map which took up most of the opposite wall and which showed the area covered by J.A.P. and the various sections. He looked at Section 9, the one in which was the potting shed. Had Krammer been there: was he still in that section?

Restlessly, he lit a cigarette, careless about the number he was smoking. Whether Krammer was trying to find his soul or even if he had a soul, what were the relative degrees of guilt, were now meaningless questions. Only one thing was of any importance. Where was Krammer? If only he, Agar, could be doing something, he thought angrily. But whereas J.A.P. had been designed to bring mobility to the various police forces, its effect on him seemed to be to have pushed him into almost complete immobility. When his instincts were to get out and do something, his orders were to stay put.

He thought about Krammer's problems. A man on the run needed food and shelter: Krammer would surely give himself away in trying to get both those. There couldn't be the remotest village store, window filled with everything from wellingtons to fly-papers, which he could enter without being instantly recognized. He would have to break into a house for food, but this breaking and entering must instantly disclose his presence.

The telephone rang and Agar answered it. Three men, wanted in connexion with the latest train robbery, had been picked up in Kent because of the greatly increased police activity. The creepers, screwsmen, blackers, drummers, and the other thousand and one types of criminals, would all be cursing and hating Krammer because they were being directly menaced on account of him. They'd rabbit on him as soon as spit in the eye of a flatty.

He wondered whether anyone in J.A.P. had listed every single breaking and entering, or attempted breaking, that had taken place the previous night. By concentrating on the potting shed which, despite the increasing weight of evidence, could easily be a false lead the real lead might be missed. Agar picked up his telephone and tried to contact Parkinson who could get on to the other four chief superintendents in J.A.P. to find out what was being done along such lines and, if nothing, to get things moving. But Parkinson was nowhere to be found. He never bloody well was, thought Agar. Creeping far too hard round the A.C.C.'s desk. He picked up the red plastic-covered notebook and searched through it until he found the page for J.A.P. Since Parkinson wasn't around, someone else must ring up the sixteen other D.I.s and get them moving.

.   .   .   .

Stoneyacre School was one of the new 'Total Stream' schools, designed to work along the lines of a public school and at the same time do away with the feelings of inferiority and frustration which the secondary and grammar schools system was said to have fostered. Sarah Bramswell was in the advanced level, which, as everybody knew—and so presumably it caused feelings of inferiority and frustration —meant that in the old days she would have gone to a grammar school. She was clever but not brilliant and inclined to be lazy, so that her full scholastic potential was seldom reached: unfortunately, she was always in the first three in class, so that she was able to point out the total lack of need for her to work any harder. She was popular with most of the girls and some of the boys had realized she was fast becoming attractive. She gave the boys little encouragement because sex still seemed very stupid to her.

During the 11.30 break—Saturday schooling with emphasis on sport had come with 'Total Stream'—when two hundred and seventy-three pupils ranged the playgrounds seeking trouble, Sarah searched for Allyson Darcy who was in the normal level of the same form. Allyson had the kind of face that appeared in Searle cartoons and was therefore noticeable, but, hard as she looked, Sarah could not see her.

'Busty,' she called out.

A girl who was very embarrassed by the speed with which one part of her body was developing came to a halt just before the stretch of macadam which the boys used for playing cricket.

'Busty, where's Allyson?'

'Got ill. Typhoid or black-water fever.'

'But . . . but she just can't be ill today.' Sarah was quite aghast. She ran her right hand through her blonde hair, but failed to untangle any of it.

'They say she's so sick she's been coughing up part of her stomach,' continued the other, with all the heartless improbability of the healthy young.

'What about the party?'

'Well. What about it?'

'Isn't Allyson going?'

'Her? The coffin's already been ordered. It's going to be very plain and cheap.'

'Her dad's driving me home after the party.'

'No he isn't, not now. Anyway, what's wrong with your dad? Crippled?'

'He's going to one of his soft meetings.'

'What's it this time? Down with toffee-eating Brazilians?'

'I don't know what it is,' said Sarah, in despair, looking utterly miserable.

'I can't see why you're all moans. You can walk home in half a second.'

'Mum won't let me walk back and that's why I told her Allyson would give me a lift.'

'Is Dotty going?'

'I'm not going to ask her. She sneaked on me and that rhyme.'

'It was rather hot,' said Busty, with a reminiscing giggle.

Two boys strolled past and began to remark upon certain of Busty's physical features. She replied with a venom that sent them away, ears red. 'Why won't your mum let you walk back?' she asked, after a while.

'It's something stupid to do with that man who's escaped from prison. When I asked them what it was he did to the girls they wouldn't tell me. Mum's stupid sometimes. I could walk back in ten minutes or a quarter of an hour, but she said I couldn't go if I had to walk and so I said Allyson's dad could bring me back, but now it looks as if Allyson isn't going.'

'Have you told anyone she isn't?'

'Don't be so stupid. How could I have told 'em when you've only just told me.'

'Then don't say anything.'

Sarah spoke slowly. 'Mum doesn't half lay into me if she catches me lying.'

'But who's lying? When you told her what was what, it couldn't have been truer. She hasn't asked you if anything's changed. So if she doesn't ask and you don't tell, you can't lie, can you?'

'I suppose that's right.'

'You're just soft, you are.'

'Who's soft?'

'You are, if you can't work that out.'

'I'm not psychologically warped,' replied Sarah, with lofty superiority.

'If you aren't, your dad is,' retorted Busty, determined to have the last word.

Six

The search for Krammer continued. Reports of his having been seen continued to come into almost every police station in the country.

Comparison tests were now being made between the thread of blue serge found in the potting shed and a thread taken from the trousers belonging to the warder from whom the coat and hat had been stolen: sight and feel had suggested they were similar. This test would not, unfortunately, be definitive, though, because there was no certainty that both the trousers and the jacket had been made from the same length of material, so that even if the two threads did not match this would not be proof that the one from the potting shed had not come from the coat Krammer was wearing: if, indeed, he was still wearing it.

Inevitably, the search was hindered because it could not be as concentrated as the police wanted. If only they could have been absolutely certain that Krammer had been in that potting shed they could have flooded the surrounding countryside with searchers: but they could not be and the whole country had to be covered.

Agar, at H.Q., correlated the reports regarding all breakings and enterings that were coming in from the D.I.s of J.A.P. When he had seen Parkinson just before lunch he had mentioned the idea and now the chief superintendent was treating the idea as if it had originally come from him. So far, the results were useless.

At 4.30 p.m. Agar leaned back in his chair. He stretched his arms above his head and yawned. Surely, Krammer must soon be recaptured, before anything happened?

.   .   .   .   .

At 4.30 p.m. Stoneyacre School broke up for the day. Boys and girls hurried out of the buildings and into the road, and then gradually dispersed as cars picked them up, they queued at bus stops, or disappeared down side streets.

Sarah walked home and found her mother in the kitchen, trying to prepare dinner for her husband who was due back at six and would be leaving the house again at seven, sharp. Betty Bramswell was a bad cook and when things went wrong she conceived the same kind of irrational hate for the food that other people felt for machines which refused to work. Sarah, who was a good cook considering her limited experience, asked her mother if she could help. Betty, complaining that the stuffing for the breasts of mutton was refusing to do what it should, pushed everything across and did not bother to ask herself why her daughter was being so helpful.

Betty lit a cigarette, and as she watched the deft hands of her daughter solve the problem of the stuffing, she slowly regained her previous good humour. 'All ready for Gwen's party, dear?'

'Yes, Mum,' replied Sarah, and she turned her face to the right so that it would not be in full view. If asked the terrible question directly she would have to tell the truth and she silently prayed—with all the fervour of a young person not really believing in the efficacy of such prayers but ready to be agreeably surprised—that her mother would not do this.

'Have you ironed your blue dress?'

'I'm going to wear the green one.'

'I don't know, love. The blue one really suits you much better.'

'But it's terribly young.'

Her mother smiled and the expression removed many of the lines of care and worry from her face. 'Are you really so very ancient, then?'

'But you know what I mean. It's . . . it looks as if it was for someone much younger than me.'

'As you like. Your father can drop you there if you're ready in time.'

'Thanks.'

'Their house is that big one with all the lovely rhododendron bushes, isn't it?'

'Yes, Mum.'

'And you say the party goes on until about eleven?'

Sarah, a note of desperation in her voice, said: 'Should I wear a ribbon in my hair, Mum?'

'I should if I were you, dear. But do make certain it matches your dress. Last time you wore a colour that positively shrieked: now what was it?'

Sarah kneaded the stuffing with her well-formed hands. At all costs she had to keep the subject of the time at which the party finished away from her mother's mind. The ribbon had been green, so she made a deliberate mistake. 'It was pink, wasn't it?'

'Pink? Somehow I don't think it was. No, definitely not pink. I'll swear you've never worn that colour in your hair. Now let me think. . . .'

She's completely forgotten about the end of the party, thought Sarah triumphantly, and whether Allyson's father's picking me up. Then she desperately tried to forget the subject herself, in case, by thought transference, her mother should return to it.

. . . . .

As twilight gradually went and night began, thousands of men all over the country stopped their search of woods, valleys, derelict buildings, hills, caves, and anywhere else that might be a hiding place for Krammer. In millions of homes all doors and windows were locked and, despite the warmth, all windows were shut.

The first wave of deep apprehension among the public had receded and had been replaced by the feeling that Krammer was not as dangerous as everyone had, at first, believed: even though, of course, it was still sense to lock the doors and windows just in case. Krammer had an appalling record, it was true, but now that he was a man on the run, with a face instantly recognizable by everyone in the country, he would not get the chance to cause trouble again.

At Gwen Bailey's party no one was thinking about Krammer. The Farm House Trio were not there—Gwen's father was not that wealthy—but there was a four-piece band whose beat-'n'-stomp music was nearly as acceptable. There were several smoochy young men who caused a great deal of amusement among the younger girls, a film show that was quite, quite corny, and a fruit punch to which, quite unknown to the hosts, had been added what one of the smoochy boys swore was pure gin.

Sharp at eleven o'clock cars began to arrive to take people home. Gwen's mother asked Sarah if she was being taken back by someone and Sarah replied that she was, since any other answer would almost certainly get back to her mother. And if that happened there would be the most terrible trouble.

At 11.12 Sarah left the house and walked down the path which ran between the rhododendron bushes. She said good-bye to one of her form-mates who was being taken home by a father who was complaining at having missed the end of his favourite TV programme.

Sarah walked along the deserted pavement. On both sides of the road the houses were, with three exceptions, in darkness. The street lighting was fairly good, but there were patches of darkness and she walked through these as quickly as she could. It was not that she was scared, she told herself, because that would have been stupid. It was just ... well ... well, at the end of the road was the common and she rather wished that the common wasn't there.

She came to the end of the road and stood still, directly under a street light. There was a T junction here and this marked the beginning of the common, which spread out on either side of the left-hand road. The tall horse-chestnut trees, with their wide-flung branches weighed down with closely packed leaves, turned everything so dark. As she stared at all this darkness, a car came down the road from the direction of London, passed her, and went on towards Stoneyacre. She noticed the strange popping noises the engine was making.

She began to talk to herself. 'The sun was shining on the sea, shining with all its might: And this was odd, because it was the middle of the night.' She felt sure she had made a mistake, but could not think where. 'Come on, Sarah, stop seeing bogey-bogeys. In no time at all you'll be home and Mum will call out and want to know what kind of a party it was and did I remember to say thank you, Mrs. Bailey, that was a wonderful party and was the food nice and the house smart? Come on, Sarah. Left foot forward and keep in time to the music. Ta-ra-ra-boom-de-ay, ta-ra-ra-boom-de-ay . . .'

51

She crossed the road to the far pavement. The street lighting continued, but the bulging mass of the chestnut trees cut off so much of it that the pools of darkness between them were big and sprawling. Nearer the lights, the shadows shivered as the trees moved to the slight breeze.

'Who's afraid of the big bad wolf?' she asked herself. She began to hop, twice on her right foot, twice on her left.

Ahead of her she saw a car that had stopped by the side of the road. The boot was very large and the rear window swept back in a very flowery fashion, and she was certain it was the car that had passed her at the corner, its engine popping. As she approached, a man shut the boot lid and stood up. There was enough light from the car and the lamp-post beyond it for her to see that he was wearing a uniform. That immediately reassured her.

'Hullo, walking home?' asked the man, as she came abreast of him.

He had a nice, kind voice and she was immediately certain that he often spoke to girls. Her parents had always taught her to go to a policeman if ever she needed help and she never for one moment thought that this man might not be wearing a policeman's uniform.

'Isn't it rather late for a young girl like you to be out on your own?'

'I don't think it's very late.'

He laughed: a nice, quiet, pleasant laugh. 'When I was your age, young lady, I was never allowed to be up at this time. How far have you got to go?'

'Only into Stoneyacre.'

'And exactly how far is that?'

'About a mile,' she answered, guessing wildly.

'I suppose it's down this road?'

'Yes.'

'I'm going that way, so I'll take you. It'll save you walking and I'm sure your legs are tired.'

She suddenly realized that if she were dropped at the house by car her mother would hear the slam of the car door and then there would never be any need to worry about her lies being found out. 'Would you mind?' she asked.

'Of course I wouldn't. Only too glad.'

He was very polite. He opened the near-side door for her. As she climbed in, his left hand touched her right arm and it seemed to her it was shaking, as if he were shivering, and that was odd because the night was so warm.

She sat down in the front seat and began to imagine she was a duchess and that one of her footmen had just closed the door for her.

The man settled himself behind the steering-wheel. 'Hasn't it been a lovely day?'

She was momentarily intrigued by the way the tone of his voice had changed: it had become funny peculiar, as if he had been sucking a sweet and got too much suck in his mouth. 'Where are you going?' she asked him.

'Quite a long way,' he said.

He reached forward to the dashboard and switched on the engine, then seemed to have trouble in finding the starter. In the end, he succeeded, but the engine twice refused to fire.

'There's something wrong with the car, isn't there?' she asked.

'Why d'you say that?'

'When you went past it sounded all popping.'

'Past where?'

'Past me earlier on. You must have seen me?'

'Yes, of course.'

'I was standing at the corner. This is a jolly comfortable car, isn't it?'

He managed to get the engine to fire and went to release the handbrake, but couldn't find it.

'Have you lost something?' she asked.

He appeared to become flustered and moved his left hand too quickly so that it crashed into the parcels shelf. He drew in his breath sharply because of the pain, but when he went to withdraw his hand he at last found the hand-brake lever. He released it.

'It's a funny car,' she said. 'I don't think I've seen one like it before. What kind is it?'

'What kind?'

'You know, what make? Is it a Ford? It looks like one with all those headlamps in front.'

'Yes, it is.'

'What kind of Ford?' She noticed that he kept looking in the rear-view mirror. 'Are you expecting someone?'

'Why d'you ask that?'

'Because you keep looking in the mirror. I thought perhaps you're on duty and looking out for someone, like on the telly.'

'Yes. That's right, I am.' He accelerated and the car surged forward, jerking repeatedly as the engine misfired. He realized the headlights were not on and began to fiddle with the switches. The windscreen wipers worked and then the engine was almost strangled as he pulled out the choke. Finally, the headlights came on. He changed gear.

'Haven't you had this car for long?' she asked, with the insatiable curiosity of youth which suffers no embarrassment from asking questions.

'No, I haven't.'

The engine began to misfire badly, so that it seemed the car was slowing down to a halt, then it gained speed once more as the engine apparently cleared itself. They reached the end of the common.

'See this place ahead on the right?' asked Sarah, a few seconds later.

'Yes.'

'Mrs. Pretty lives there. She's batty: but completely. Hardly ever goes out and she shoots anyone who goes in her garden except for the old gardener and he's a batty as her. We call her Ugly-Pugly. My father went there one day to try to get her to join one of his stupid things and she cursed him and tried to throw water over him: at least that's what he says and he's usually truthful even if the person does have a lot of money. He says a lot of money is terrible, but it doesn't seem to have done much harm to Gwen.'

There were now houses on either side of the road, houses which did not stand in their own large gardens.

'That's my house, by the third lamp-post,' she said, 'on the right. Mum's still awake, up in the bedroom. Dad's out at his silly meeting still, but I s'pect he'll be back soon.'

He accelerated and the engine note rose. A car which was coming in the opposite direction flashed its light at them, but he did not try to dip.

'That's my house you've just gone past,' said Sarah loudly.

They reached the cross-roads which divided up Stoney-acre both physically and socially, so that the individual homes were to the north and the housing estates to the south.

'You've gone past my home,' repeated Sarah. 'I want to get out.'

He made no answer. A lorry, belching diesel fumes out of its exhaust, passed in the opposite direction and it flashed its headlights at them when he did not dip.

She was becoming a little panicky. As yet, she had not

realized the truth: she just thought that this 'policeman' had suddenly gone a bit queer. 'I must get out!' she shouted above the noise of the engine, which once more had begun to splutter and cough.

He cursed as he pumped the accelerator up and down without effect and the engine seemed to be about to die.

She began to wind down the window, without any clear idea of what she intended to do. He took his left hand off the steering-wheel and swept it round, hitting her in the throat. Pain streaked through her neck and she choked violently.

For several seconds, while her mind was shocked, she tried to overcome the agony in her throat. When that had eased a bit she realized the car had stopped and that the man had turned round sideways and was looking at her. An oncoming car's headlights filled the interior of the car with light and she could see his face, under the peaked cap, quite clearly. The eyes now seemed to be wild: almost mad were the words that occurred to her. The face suddenly became frighteningly familiar. Even though he was in uniform, this was Krammer, the man who had escaped from jail.

Her bewildered mind told her that she had to escape, no matter what. No one in her form at school really knew what this man had done to those girls he had killed, but they had gone through all the possibilities that occurred to them and had frightened themselves with the horrible things they thought up.

She twisted round and reached for the handle of the door. Two hands gripped her throat and squeezed. At first she struggled to tear his hands free, then she couldn't do anything because of the blinding pain. Her eyeballs seemed to be about to burst and her chest was white-hot with agony. The pain rose to a paralysing crescendo and then, mercifully, vanished as she collapsed into unconsciousness.

Krammer let go of her throat. He remained motionless, except for his hands which were shaking, until a car came up behind, drew out, and passed. The glare of the headlights seemed to jerk his mind back into action.

He took a handkerchief from his pocket and used it to gag the girl. With a strength that was unusual for anyone with a build like his, he lifted the girl up over the back of the seat and dropped her on to the 'occasional' seats behind. He took some string from his pocket and tied her wrists together and then her wrists to her ankles. There was a travelling rug which he used to cover her.

As he sat back in the driving seat, he trembled violently. After the spasm had passed he shook himself as a man does who is bewildered and tries to force some comprehension into his consciousness. He took a packet of cigarettes from the coat pocket and lit one.

After a while he drove on. The engine began to get very much worse, so that the car jerked badly. He tried changing gear rapidly, up and then down, revving hard, and for a while this appeared to clear up the trouble, but ten minutes later it was back. By now they were a long way out from Stoneyacre, in the middle of countryside, with grass verges and thorn hedges on either side. He was wondering what he would do if the engine stopped altogether when he saw ahead a blur of lights that could only mean an all-night garage. He pulled his peaked cap well down on his head and drove into the garage forecourt.

The attendant had been sleeping in a small hut, to the right of the blacked-out showroom, but a bell, activated by a small air-filled rubber tube over which the car had run, brought him outside, yawning. He went up to the petrol pumps.

Krammer lowered the window. 'The engine's misfiring very badly,' he called out.

The attendant shrugged his shoulders. 'There ain't a mechanic on the place.'

'Can't you do something?'

'I'm not a mechanic, mister. Tell you what, though. I'll have a look in case there's something simple. Open up the bonnet.'

As he felt around the dashboard, Krammer cursed. He had no idea where the bonnet release catch was on this car. If he couldn't operate it at once the man would come round and try to find it himself and then would almost certainly see Krammer's face sufficiently well to recognize it.

By sheer luck he found the catch and released the bonnet.

He sat back and lit another cigarette, careful to shield his face as the attendant lifted the bonnet and peered into the engine. He thought he heard a sound from behind and turned until he could look over the seat. The travelling rug remained motionless.

The attendant stood up and pushed the bonnet down until it clicked shut. 'You're lucky, mister, it was only a loose plug lead.'

'How much is that?'

'Let's call it nothing. Like I said, I ain't no mechanic so I don't charge no mechanic's wages.'

The attendant expected to be tipped, but to his angry surprise the window of the car was wound up, the engine was started, and the car was driven off. Outraged, he cursed the world where he did a man a favour and in return merely got a kick where it hurt. The next time someone wanted something done in the middle of the night, he told himself, that person could go whistle.

Krammer returned to the road and increased speed. At first everything was all right, then after little more than a couple of minutes the engine began coughing again. He stopped the car, released the bonnet catch, and climbed out.

The plug leads were all in position. He cursed the petrol-pump attendant for a lying incompetent.

Where was he to go? He must find somewhere safe, but was anywhere safe for him? He had picked up an evening paper thrown away into a litter basket and had seen his photograph on the front page and then had read the description of the tremendous man-hunt now going on. He must have found somewhere safe for himself and the girl by daylight.

Often, he knew, his thoughts became a little muddled when he was troubled or excited, but now he was able to keep them quite clear. The problem was simply put. The car was only just limping along, and might, at any time, pack up and so leave him stranded, yet he must, somehow, find security.

Very suddenly he remembered Mrs. Ugly-Pugly, the mad woman who threw water at people. She lived on her own and never allowed anyone near the house. She could offer him sanctuary.

Would the car go back that far? He switched on and started the engine and this time, just to prove its perversity, it ran smoothly. He made a U turn and began to drive back. Within two minutes the engine was popping again.

The headlights showed up the woods lining the road on his left and separated from it only by a narrow grass verge. He decided the woods would suit his purpose and braked the car to a halt, then switched off headlights and engine.

He left the car and went round to the boot. He lifted the lid and, after a quick visual check to make certain there were no other cars on the road, he dragged out the unconscious man. Blood covered most of the right-hand side of the man's face and as his head moved more blood trickled out of a wound under his hair.

Krammer carried the man into the woods and dropped

59

him into a convenient hollow. He threw dead leaves on to him until the light of the torch, which he had found in the car, showed that the man was covered.

When he returned to the car and sat down there was a muffled groan from the rear. He twisted round and saw that the girl was moving under the blanket. He drew the blanket back and looked down at her. 'Don't worry,' he said. 'There's no need to worry.'

She stared up at him with a terror that was still deadened by the shock of what she had already suffered.

He reached over the seat until he could put his right hand on her exposed leg. 'There's no need to worry,' he repeated.

She tried to jerk her leg away, but his hand prevented her. She felt the fingers stroke her flesh for a couple of seconds, then he let go. He pulled the rug back over her. She heard the engine start and felt the car jerk forward.

Seven

Charles Bramswell drove the mini-van into the garage and switched off engine and lights. He opened the door and swore as it scraped the brick wall. If a mini-van hardly fitted into the garage what did the builders think would have been the situation had he been able to afford a decent-sized car? He laughed harshly. Had he been able to afford a decent-sized car, he would not have lived in a house called Terawana. When they had first moved into the house he had thought the name attractive, but later he had discovered that it was the Makolkol equivalent of Hillside. You couldn't get more surburban than that.

He went into the kitchen. The electric clock said almost midnight, which surprised him. The meeting must have gone on longer than he had supposed, as did so many meetings these days: being a partially self-honest man he knew that one of the reasons for this was that, as chairman, he had not given a nearly definite enough lead because he was finding it more and more difficult to decide what lead he wanted to give. Except for the left-wing ones, the papers always referred to the association in the most derisory terms, refusing to admit the possibility of honest beliefs and interests. Until recently he had never doubted either. Yet now . . . Why, he asked himself angrily as he poured out a glass of milk, did a man begin to lose faith with his ideals? How could one's certainties of the verities of a true way of life suffer a change?

He went upstairs and into their bedroom. Betty was asleep, her face turned away from the bedside light, which was still switched on. She looked young and pretty: he was reminded of their wedding day when he had worn his officer's uniform with its pocketful of fivers. Those were the days of honest, aristocratic fivers, white, black, and crinkly, regarded with suspicion by shopkeepers. These days shopkeepers handled fivers without thinking: only he seldom had one to give them.

He leaned over and kissed her. She turned, opened her eyes, and looked at him. He kissed her again.

'Hullo, Knobbly,' she said softly.

That had been his nickname during the war, bestowed in honour of the shape of his knees.

After a while she spoke again. 'Get into bed.'

'With my shoes on?'

'What's it matter if everything else is off?'

He began to undress quickly, throwing his clothes on to the chair at the foot of the bed.

'Would you just see Sarah's all right, darling?'

'O.K.' He crossed to the door, then stopped. 'Don't fall asleep before I get back.'

She smiled.

He went out and across the small landing, with its carpet worn in the centre, to the opposite bedroom. He knocked softly on the door and when there was no answer he slowly opened it and looked inside. The light from the landing was enough to show that the bed was empty.

He returned to Betty. 'She's not back yet,' he said.

'Not? What's the time?'

'Almost a quarter past twelve.'

She sat up. 'Sarah said the party ended at eleven.'

'There's no need to flap, I expect it just carried on. You know what they are these days, a couple of those awful

62

records by a band of juvenile delinquents and the young will keep going until it's daybreak.'

'But she knows how I'd start worrying the moment she was late.'

'Considering you were fast asleep, I don't think you were worrying all that hard.' He took off his shoes.

'Charles, go to the Baileys' house and bring her back, will you?'

'Look, Betty, you know what they're like——'

'Are you going, or shall I?'

He looked at her. 'I will.' He put his shoes back on and tied the laces.

She had expected him to argue and when he didn't she felt a warm flush of gratitude. Damn Sarah, she thought angrily. Normally irritable when he had returned from one of his meetings, this time he had been in the kind of mood she had for so long wanted to rediscover. Had he been able to get into bed and make love with her it could so easily have begun something fresh which an effort on both their parts would have kept alive. 'Charles.'

'Yes.'

'Hurry back as quickly as you can.'

He kissed her again. 'Madam, you're acting like a houri.'

'Are you aware that houris are not ladies of easy virtue?'

'My ideal of a houri is.' He grinned, then walked across to the door. He recognized the fact that something which would normally have infuriated him was now not doing so.

He went downstairs and out to the garage. He backed the van on to the road and wondered whether he was causing the old bitch next door to swallow her false teeth in the excitement of trying to work out what was going on.

He took the London road across the common and then turned right. Bailey's house was in the fashionable part of

63

Stoneyacre and he made the kind of money which enabled him to employ a full-time gardener and open his gardens to the public twice a year. Bramswell turned off the road into the curving drive that was bordered by rhododendron bushes and then rose beds. When he came in sight of the house he saw that it was in complete darkness and there were no cars parked outside.

For the first time he began to feel uneasy. The party was over and clearly had been for some time, so why wasn't Sarah home?

The drive circled a large flower bed and he followed it round and back to the road, where he stopped to try to sort out things. What was the name of the person who had been giving Sarah a lift home? At first his mind refused to recall it, then it suggested Allyson. But Allyson who? Betty would know, but he didn't want to worry her at this stage because she was the kind of person who thought of tetanus the moment any of her family suffered the slightest cut. Yet unless he could remember Allyson's surname . . . He couldn't and he had to drive home.

When he entered their bedroom it was quite plain just how much Betty had been worrying. Her voice was sharp. 'Why have you been so long?'

'I was as quick as I could be.'

'Is she here now?'

'No.'

'Then where in God's name is she?'

'I don't quite know . . .'

'What about the party? Why didn't you go on in and get her out of it?'

'The house was in darkness. The party must have been over for some time.'

'Then . . . then where is she?'

'She must have gone home with Allyson for a drink of

cocoa or something else hot. I'd have gone to get her from there, but I couldn't remember Allyson's surname or where she lives.'

'Then Mr. Bailey saw her leave with Allyson and Allyson's father?'

'I don't know.'

'Why?'

'I didn't wake the Baileys up.'

'Why not? What was the use of going there if you didn't?'

This could so easily have slipped into becoming one of the interminable and bitter wrangles that so often occurred, but for once he remained patient, knowing how desperately worried she was. 'Sarah must have gone back with Allyson, so I'll go and check. What's the name?'

'Darcy and they live out at Tincton, which is at least eight miles from here. They'd never have driven Sarah all that way just for a cup of cocoa. Charles, something must have happened.'

Would anyone drive eight miles out, eight miles back, and finally a further eight miles home, just to give a young girl a cup of something warm which she could so easily have in her own home? He knew it to be a quite illogical explanation even as he refused to believe it impossible because it offered hope.

'Charles. D'you think it could be Krammer? Do you?'

'No, no, of course not, Betty.'

'Oh God, Charles, I couldn't live if that happened. Please, Charles, it can't be that, can it?'

'Krammer isn't anywhere within a hundred miles of here and even if he were Sarah's ten times too sensible a kid to let herself be caught by him. Krammer won't be worrying about anything but keeping clear of the police and for all we know he may already have been captured and shoved back in prison.'

'I'm going to come with you.' She pulled back the bed-clothes and stood up. Her nylon nightdress was transparent enough to show that her figure was almost as fashionably slim as it had been when they had married. She dressed with a frantic hurry, putting on a cardigan inside out.

They went down and out to the van. 'Whereabouts in Tincton?' he asked, as he started the engine.

'Just at the back of the church. I took Sarah to a party there last year.' She spoke in a tight, clipped voice, desperately trying to keep her racing fears in check. Her imagination kept trying to picture Sarah in the hands of Krammer, suffering some of the things those other girls had suffered.

He drove the van as fast as it would go and Betty said nothing, although she was normally a very nervous passenger. They reached the small village and its ancient stone-built church, skirted the graveyard with its crumbling tombstones, and after one wrong turning found the Darcys' house.

They had been desperately hoping to find the lights on in the house and a car parked outside, waiting to drive Sarah home. But the place was in darkness and there was no car.

He braked the car to a halt and switched off. She searched for his hand and when she took hold of it he could feel that she was trembling.

'We'll go and ask them what happened,' he said, trying to keep his voice level.

'Maybe . . . maybe she's sleeping here and they thought it was too late to ring us tonight, but were going to first thing in the morning?' she muttered desperately.

'Maybe.' It couldn't be, he knew. No parents could ever be so stupid as to act like that. God in hell, what had happened to Sarah?

They walked up the crazy-paving path to the front door and he rang the electric bell. After a while he rang it again.

He had a sudden, desperate desire to smoke and searched in his pockets for some cigarettes. He cursed when he couldn't find any.

There was a leaded semicircle of glass above the front door and this suddenly filled with light. They heard approaching footsteps.

'Who is it?' a man's voice called out.

'Charles Bramswell.'

'Who?'

'Charles Bramswell, Sarah's father. My wife's here with me.'

After two bolts were withdrawn the door was opened. Darcy stood on the mat just inside and stared at them. He was a small man, belligerent in appearance and nature. 'We were very fast asleep, my wife and I,' he snapped.

'Where's Sarah?' asked Betty desperately.

'I have no idea.'

'But . . . but you drove her back from the Baileys' party.'

'I most certainly did not. I have not left the house at all tonight.'

Betty's face was white and strained. 'You must have done. Please, you must have done.'

Darcy's anger was finally dispelled as he realized the full extent of the anguish of the two Bramswells. 'You'd better come in so that we can see what's what.'

'But Sarah . . .' she began.

'Let's go in,' muttered Charles Bramswell hoarsely. He took hold of her left arm and almost pushed her inside.

Darcy led them into the sitting-room. He pointed at the comfortable chairs and then crossed to an elaborately inlaid cocktail cabinet, with ball and claw feet, and opened one of the doors. 'Something strong?'

'I can't drink anything,' said Betty.

'Whisky, please,' said Charles. 'For both of us.'

'How did Allyson get back from the party?' demanded Betty. 'Surely you fetched her?'

Darcy looked quickly at her. 'She didn't go.' He poured out three drinks. 'She's been in bed for the past two days with a really heavy cold.'

Betty put her right forefinger to her lips as though trying to stop their trembling. 'Sarah said . . . She told us you were driving her back to our house when it was over.'

Darcy came across to where they sat and handed each of them a glass. 'What can Bailey tell you?'

Charles stared at him for several seconds before answering. 'I drove straight to their house, but there wasn't a light on anywhere so I was certain you'd brought her away. We . . . we thought you must have driven her back here.'

'The first thing to do, then, is to telephone the Baileys.'

'Yes, of course.'

'I'll do it for you.' Darcy left the room.

Betty drank without tasting what she was drinking. She was struggling to keep calm, desperately fighting to prevent her mind slipping into a nightmare of terror. Yet it was a losing battle in which Charles' support was not enough to prevent her imagining Sarah in the hands of Krammer, suffering as those other girls had suffered. . . .

Darcy returned to the room. It was obvious that, for once, he was reluctant to speak. 'I had a word with Bailey,' he finally said. 'As far as he knows, Sarah left at the end of the party. Mrs. Bailey asked Sarah if someone was taking her and Sarah said someone was, but neither of them has any idea who it was.' He looked first at Betty, then at Charles Bramswell—a man whom he had always disliked and despised. Now his only feeling was one of intense and bitter sorrow for both of them and an equally intense gratitude that Allyson was upstairs, asleep. He coughed, almost nervously. 'Don't you think it would be a good idea to phone the police?'

.   .   .   .   .

Mrs. Pretty's surname amused a great number of people —was there anyone in the world so hilariously, inaccurately named? She was thickset, almost plump, and she had a square, ugly face. She abstained from using any make-up, the last time she had worn lipstick was just before her husband died, and she cut her own hair, badly, with a large pair of dress-making scissors. Her clothes, once of good quality, had become shabby: sometimes she bothered to repair them, sometimes she didn't. Most of the villagers were agreed that she was not entitled to the Mrs. in front of her name since nobody like her could ever have persuaded a man to marry her. Most of the villagers had no idea what kind of a person she really was. She had been ardently courted and ardently married by a man who thought her very attractive. Her nature was essentially an emotional one and she was sexually very much alive. Their marriage had been a rare combination of complete happiness and mutual sexual satisfaction, so that instincts which had always been strong within her were allowed to flower most luxuriantly. Yet, looking at her fifteen years after her husband had died in a car accident, it was almost impossible to visualize all the things that her marriage had meant to her.

She was wealthy. Her husband had left her a considerable sum of money and one of his very close friends managed her finances for her: he had made certain that the value of her fortune outstripped the rate of depreciation of money. Even the latest tax on capital had not affected her as badly as it had so many people because she was expertly advised to take full advantage of the escape clause in the Act.

When her husband was killed she had wanted to die as well, but she just failed to have sufficient courage or cowardice to commit suicide. She moved to Stoneyacre with her grief and because she had no children she lived too much with that grief. She became a recluse. Adults thought she was queer in the head and children were certain she was a witch.

For fifteen years her life went on monotonously and almost as if time and an outside world did not exist. Then, at 12.43 a.m., Sunday the 18th of July, the world suddenly came to her and harshly reminded her of its existence.

She was asleep in her bedroom on the upstairs floor of the old Victorian rectory. On the grained marble mantelpiece above the fireplace was the studio photograph of her late husband, and on the dressing-table, which he had bought for her in an antique shop in Brighton, were three framed photographs of him which she had taken on their honeymoon. The photographs had become yellow with age and they were all slightly out of focus.

There was the clattering noise of breaking glass and she awoke.

As she lay in the bed, she wondered what had awakened her. Had there been a crash on the road as had once happened or had the wind blown a door shut? But there were no other sounds from the road and there had hardly been any wind earlier on and certainly there was no more now or the leaves of the trees would be rustling.

A stair creaked. It was the fourth from the bottom and it always creaked when anyone stepped on it.

She was very afraid, but she managed to overcome that fear. Where another woman might have lain in bed shivering from fright, she climbed out on to the floor and, treading very carefully so as not to make the bedroom floorboards creak, she crossed the room to the small Chippendale desk.

In the top drawer was an old Webley revolver, used by her late husband in the Abyssinian War. He had taught her how to load it and fire it with reasonable accuracy.

The excitement of fear made her heart race, but she held the revolver steady as she went over to the door and then stood still, listening. She heard footsteps go past her room and seconds later there was a smothered cry as someone knocked into the ugly cast-iron doorstop that stood halfway along the landing. She was almost certain it had been a woman or a girl who had cried out. She made up her mind to run from her room to the stairs, down them, and along the hall to the telephone. No one could get near her while she had the gun in her hand.

Immediately outside the bedroom door was the switch for the landing lights. She unlocked the door, opened it, switched on the main light, and stepped out. As she did so, she realized that she was wearing nothing but a cotton nightdress.

She ran to the head of the stairs and then looked along the far corridor. A man stepped out of the bedroom in which she kept all the clothes that had belonged to her late husband at the time of his death. As she watched, he dragged a girl out of the room.

She cocked the gun with her thumb and held it down by her side. They stared at each other, momentarily wondering what to do next.

'Help. Please, please help me,' Sarah screamed and tried to jerk her wrist free. 'He said he'd just drive me home. He's that terrible man who killed those girls. You've got to help me.'

Mrs. Pretty wondered for a moment if the girl were mad. This man, of medium height, almost slender, dressed in a uniform, looked far too ordinary to be the sex maniac. Then he moved slightly and the light cut under the peak of his cap to show his face more distinctly and she knew with frightening certainty that this was Krammer.

He put his right arm right round Sarah's neck and squeezed. She screamed again and the screams continued until cut off by the pressure on her throat.

Mrs. Pretty suddenly felt sick. That sound hurt her somewhere deep inside. She and her late husband had longed for children, but had had none. Had she had a daughter, she would have wished her to be like this tall, attractive, blonde-haired girl whom the man was treating so brutally.

'I don't want to hurt her,' said Krammer. 'I promise you, I don't want to hurt her.' He began to move forward, very slowly, keeping his arm round Sarah's neck, but not so tightly as it had been. His pale blue eyes watched the revolver.

Mrs. Pretty tried desperately to decide what to do to help this poor, tortured girl. If she fired now she could so easily hit the girl: in any case, did she have the courage to shoot him, just like that and when he was not actually attacking her? If she made any other move, and it failed, he was going to strangle the girl.

When only feet away, Krammer suddenly put his right knee in the middle of Sarah's back and at the same time he let go of her throat. She was thrown forward to crash into Mrs. Pretty. Mrs. Pretty was hit in the stomach and she gasped from the sudden pain of the blow. Then, before she had time to force her body into action, her right wrist was seized and twisted violently. Involuntarily, she fired the revolver and the violent noise beat at all their eardrums: the air was filled with the acrid stench of the burnt charge. She struggled to free her hand, but the strength of the man was tremendous and the agony of the grip so great that she had to let go of the gun.

Sarah, tears streaking down her cheeks, suddenly dropped towards the floor and managed to drag herself free. She raced for the stairs, reached them and was down to the small half-landing when her foot caught in a torn patch of carpet and she fell over, crashed into the banisters, and lay where she fell, almost completely winded.

Krammer broke the gun and emptied the cartridges into his hand, then dropped them into his right-hand coat pocket. 'I don't want to do anything to hurt her, I promise you,' he said, with even more earnestness than before. 'But I shall have to, if you try to do anything. You do understand that, don't you? You see, if you . . .' His voice trailed off into silence.

Mrs. Pretty was abruptly possessed of a terrible blasphemous thought. Krammer's eyes were very much like her late husband's had been: very light blue, almost slate coloured, and set wide apart.

Krammer walked round her and went down the stairs to the half-landing. He held out his hand to Sarah. 'Come on, Sarah, I'll give you a heave up.'

She gave a whimpering sound and tried to retreat, but was prevented from moving by the banisters which were hard up against her back.

'Please be helpful,' said Krammer, in his soft, calm voice. 'You see, if you are helpful I won't have to hurt you any more.' He bent down until he could take hold of Sarah's right hand and he carefully brought her up to her feet. He turned and spoke to Mrs. Pretty. 'She's terribly tired and. needs a lot of rest. Can we put her to sleep in a spare bed? And after that I must put my car in the garage.'

Mrs. Pretty forced herself to think calmly, to treat this man as if he were sane and his requests were sane, and to do everything to put him off his guard so that she could find a chance to escape and bring help. 'As you don't want to hurt her it would be so much kinder to let her go home,' she said pleadingly.

Sarah began to struggle. She tried to get her mouth down to his hand so that she could bite it, but without seeming to exert very much force he hooked his arm under her chin and held her head upright.

'You've got to help me!' screamed Sarah. 'He strangled me in the car. Please, please do something. Please get me back to Mummy.' She was too young to realize fully the horror of the position she was in or the mentality of the man, but she did know enough to be terrified.

'Take her back home,' pleaded Mrs. Pretty.

'I can't,' he answered very seriously. 'I swear that's the truth. I can't.'

'If you let her go back to her home . . .'

'She can't go until——' He cut his words short and it was obvious he was not going to say anything more.

'Until what?' she asked shrilly.

He shook his head. 'She must go to bed. She's tired.'

Sarah struggled again and he applied pressure to her throat so that he began to strangle her. Remembering the blinding agony that had swept over her when he had throttled her into unconsciousness in the car, she now became motionless. She began to cry and the deep sobbing shook her body. He relaxed his hold.

'Which bedroom shall we take her to?' he asked.

'There aren't any beds made up. No one ever stays here. Can't you see she must go back home?'

'Which is the most comfortable bed?'

'Let her sleep with me. She'll be so much more comfortable.'

'I wish I could, but you might try to help her to escape. She's got to stay here until——' For the second time he stopped short at that word. After a pause he continued.

74

'She must have a comfortable bed to help her. She'll feel wonderful after a good night's sleep.'

Certain that for the moment there was nothing else she could do, Mrs. Pretty turned and walked to one of the bedrooms to the right of the stairs. She caught herself wondering whether her nightdress was at all transparent. Oh God, she thought desperately, what was she going to do? What was she going to do to help the kid? Only one thing was certain. At the moment Krammer really seemed concerned about treating Sarah decently—whatever she, Amelia Pretty did, she must not upset him one jot in case that changed his attitude.

As she opened the bedroom door, she frantically wondered what he meant by his continued use of the word 'until'. Until what?

Eight

Agar was a very deep sleeper, to the annoyance of Caroline who knew little in life as infuriating as lying in bed after having been awoken by something and to have to listen to his deep, regular, untroubled breathing. When the telephone rang in the middle of Saturday night and catapulted her into bewildered wakefulness she could have kicked him hard for going on sleeping. A telephone call at such an hour must mean trouble: was it a police call or did it concern their son? The telephone went on ringing and her husband went on sleeping. In the end she switched on the bedside lamp, climbed out of bed, put on slippers and dressing-gown, and left the room. The slight snore from her husband seemed, to her fury, to be a derisory gesture.

She went down the stairs to the telephone, which was by the hall window, lifted the receiver and said: 'Yes?' with an urgent note in her voice which showed how worried she was that this concerned her son.

'County police, Sergeant Quorn speaking, Mrs. Agar. Sorry to bother you at this time. Could I have a word with the inspector, please?'

'You'll have to wait a minute.' She returned upstairs and shook her husband with slightly more force than was strictly necessary. When he was awake he was uncharitable enough to ask her whether she couldn't have taken a message. Her answer was blunt.

He made his way downstairs and picked up the receiver. 'What the hell's the panic?'

'Quorn here, sir. There's a report that a girl's missing from Stoneyacre. The parents say she went to a party and should have been back at eleven, but there's been no sign of her yet.'

Agar twisted his wrist round and looked at his watch. It was 12.54. One hour and fifty-four minutes since she had been expected home. Quite suddenly he was fully awake. 'Krammer?'

'There's nothing to say it's him, sir. Likewise, there's nothing to say it isn't.'

'What about that report from Ilford?'

'That was declared a false alarm a couple of hours back, sir.'

'How old's the kid?'

'Just gone twelve.'

'God!' he muttered. His voice became angry. 'What the hell were the parents doing? Did they let her go home on her own? Why didn't they watch her like hawks? Did they think we kept sending out warnings for the fun of it?'

'They must be the kind of parents who never think.'

Both men were experiencing the same bitter, frustrating, useless hate for people who were too proud, stupid, or unthinking, to accept the police warnings.

Agar spoke first. 'What's moving?'

'Q Division in the field and H.Q. has put out a stand-by order to all other divisions. Mr. Parkinson says will you work with the D.I. who's heading straight for the parents' place which is in London Road. It's called Terawana. Apparently it's before the cross-roads going towards the coast.'

'O.K.'

'All right, sir.'

77

'Let's pray it's a false alarm and we find the kid's got back home by the time I get there.'

'Yes, sir. But two hours is a long time to be adrift.'

Agar replaced the telephone on its cradle and went upstairs. Caroline was sitting up in bed, resting her back against the oak headboard. 'What's the trouble, Bill?'

'There's a twelve-year-old kid been missing for two hours in Stoneyacre.'

'Oh, no!' She drew in her breath sharply. 'Not him?'

He shrugged his shoulders as he hurriedly began to dress. 'No one knows yet. The kid went to a party and was due home around eleven, but hasn't arrived. I don't know how she was supposed to be getting back, but it sounds as if it was on her own.'

'Surely no parents would let their daughter be out at night on her own when they know Krammer's loose?'

'People are twice as damned stupid as you ever reckon in your most pessimistic moments. I'm going to Stoneyacre and it's a case of seeing you when I see you.'

'Bill, Krammer's on the run. He knows every single person in the country's looking for him. Surely he wouldn't get hold of another girl and . . .'

'Wouldn't he?'

'Then . . . then you've got to find him.'

'D'you imagine any of us have been hanging back?'

'I didn't mean it like that, Bill.'

His voice became quieter. 'I know just how it is, Carry. It's the feeling any ordinary, decent human being has when he thinks what Krammer did to those other girls and what he may be doing right now to this one. It's the feeling anyone has at the thought of not finding the girl for four days.'

'Why four?'

'That's about how long it took for him to kill the other girls.'

'It's . . . it's . . .'

'It's being caught up in something one just can't understand and tries not to believe because it's so inhumanly beastly. And the chaplain said he was certain Krammer was genuinely repentant,' he ended bitterly.

'But it might still not be him?'

'Maybe not,' he agreed. But, like Sergeant Quorn, he kept thinking that the girl was two hours overdue.

He finished dressing, went downstairs, left the house, and drove his car out of the garage. He went into the centre of Carriford and picked up the London/Raleton road at the traffic lights. For a while the road was bounded by a typically ugly and depressing jumble of houses, shops, garages, builders' yards, and decaying cinemas, and then he reached the countryside. The headlights picked out green fields, haystacks, corn fields, cattle and sheep, and one unconcerned fox which crossed the road immediately in front of his car. He reached Stoneyacre in twenty-five minutes, which meant the car had been pushed harder than it should have been.

He slowed down as he approached the cross-roads and was able to identify the house, Terawana, by the lights on inside and the two cars parked outside. He noted, almost subconsciously, that it was an ugly, detached place, with a kind of squashed-in and mean appearance. When he had parked his car and climbed out on to the pavement he could see, even in the street lighting, that the house was in urgent need of decoration. He knocked on the front door, which was opened by a uniformed constable.

' 'Evening, sir,' said the constable, recognizing him, although Agar didn't know the constable.

'Any news?'

'No, sir, none.'

Agar swore. During the drive he had all but persuaded

himself that on arrival he would find this was a false alarm. The sound of voices came from the room on the right of the staircase and he went in there. Betty Bramswell, her face stained by tears, was sitting in one of the worn armchairs: behind her stood a white-faced Charles Bramswell, whom Agar vaguely knew to be some sort of trouble-maker. Sitting in the second armchair was Detective Inspector Raydon, a smallish, precise man. Also present were a detective sergeant and a detective constable.

Raydon looked round. 'Hullo, Bill. Mr. and Mrs. Bramswell, this is Detective Inspector Agar.'

They looked at Agar with desperate hope, as if, being a newcomer, he might suddenly work miracles, yet also with a bitter hopelessness, showing how little they believed in their own hope.

'Why aren't you doing something?' burst out Betty Bramswell suddenly. 'Instead of standing there, why in the name of God aren't you out looking for her?'

'A lot of people are doing that,' said Raydon gently.

'That doesn't stop you going as well. Why won't you let us go out and look if you won't? She's my daughter. Can you understand that? My daughter. I'm going mad, sitting here, thinking of what may be happening to her. Those other girls . . .'

'There's absolutely no certainty that Krammer has anything to do with your daughter's disappearance.'

She looked at Raydon and her eyes filled with fresh tears which spilled down her cheeks. 'Do you think it isn't him?'

'I don't know yet.' He looked away from her as he spoke.

Charles Bramswell rested both hands on her shoulders and stroked the sides of her neck with his thumbs in an unselfconscious gesture of loving help. She reached up with her right hand and gripped one of his.

Raydon continued with his questioning. 'She told you that Allyson Darcy's parents would drive her home? Yet when you spoke to the parents earlier tonight they made it quite clear that the day before it was certain Allyson would not be going and your daughter must have known this?'

'Yes,' said Bramswell.

'If you'd known the Darcys wouldn't have been meeting their daughter would you have let Sarah go to the party?'

'Of course we wouldn't!' cried Betty.

'You wouldn't have fetched her yourself?' The D.I. spoke to Bramswell.

'I . . . I had to be out at a meeting,' he replied hoarsely.

'You wouldn't have come away from it a bit early in order to pick her up?'

'Goddamn it, what does that matter?'

'I'm trying to discover Sarah's state of mind.'

Bramswell groaned. How unimportant that meeting now was, he thought wildly, how criminally unimportant.

'She knew, then, that you couldn't fetch her?' persisted the D.I.

Bramswell nodded.

'You told her so?'

'I said she couldn't go to the party unless someone was driving her home,' said Betty brokenly.

Agar lit a cigarette. It was cruel, bitter, and bloody work having to exacerbate the terrible feelings of the parents, reminding them how tragically selfish they had been, underlining how easily this could have been avoided, but it had to be done. It now seemed clear that Sarah had begun to walk home. She had lied to her parents about the lift Allyson Darcy's father was giving her because if she had not lied she would not have been allowed to go to the party: also, she had not asked the Baileys to take her home because, if she had, word of this would probably have got back to her parents and then she would have been in trouble.

Agar spoke to Raydon. 'Don, would it help any if I go and see the Darcys?'

Raydon looked at him. 'It might. Will you want anyone?'

'Not at the moment.' Agar left the room, after getting the address from Bramswell, and went out to his car. The night was warm and there were no clouds in the sky, so that the stars were brilliant pin-pricks of light throughout the whole black semicircle. The harsh shriek of an owl came from not far away and as he climbed into the car he thought he heard the barking of a fox.

He drove as quickly as the worn-out engine would allow. He did not expect to learn anything from the Darcys, but there was one chance in a thousand he might be wrong and in a case like this odds of a million to one were worth while. Never would he forget the agonized expression on the mother's face.

　　·　　　　·　　　　·　　　　·　　　　·

Mrs. Pretty watched Krammer as he came out of the spare bedroom, shut the door, turned the key in the lock, and pocketed the key.

'She's so very tired,' said Krammer. 'She'll sleep like a log.'

She stepped forward and spoke and her voice was low and urgent. 'Please, please listen to me. She's a lovely gay little girl from a happy home. By now her parents will be frantic. I'm sure you don't really want to cause such terrible misery, so please, I beg you, please let her go. I swear that if you do that I won't tell the police anything.'

'I can't,' he replied.

'Why not?'

'Because I just can't, not yet.' He leaned against the locked door. 'What's your Christian name?'

'My . . . my Christian name?'

'I'd like to know.'

He was so calm and peaceful and she knew that, no matter what, she had to keep him in this mood. 'Amelia.'

'That's a very lovely name. It makes me think of flowering cherry trees in the spring.'

She gasped.

He looked puzzled. 'What's the matter?'

'It . . . it's just that you've said something very like what my . . . what someone else said a long time ago. Why can't you let the girl go?'

'I promise you I'll explain everything as soon as possible.'

'But surely you can understand how terrified her parents will be?'

'Amelia, I promise you Sarah will be all right in the end. I'm looking after her to make really certain. The bed was comfortable and she said herself how soft the pillows are. I asked her whether she'd like anything to eat or drink, but the only thing she wanted was some water. I think she may have eaten a little too much at the party. Girls do do that, don't they?'

'What are you going to do?'

'Stay here with her for a little while. You'll help me look after her, won't you?'

She had to struggle hard to force her mind not to slip into believing that the situation was normal, so hypnotic was the effect of the way he was behaving and talking. 'I'll do what I can,' she answered.

'Thank you. Thank you, really. I'm going to call you Amelia if you don't mind?'

'No, I . . . I'd like that.'

'Let's go to bed now, Amelia. I'm tired and I'm sure you

83

are. I'll go to sleep in the empty bedroom next to Sarah's. I had a quick look and saw the bed with some blankets folded up on it.'

'Wouldn't you like some sheets?'

'I don't think so. We never had sheets in prison and I seem to have got out of the habit of them.'

She struggled to think of something to do, and failed. 'Then I'll go into my room.'

'Amelia, you won't try to do anything I wouldn't like, will you? I don't want to have to be nasty to you.'

He smiled at her and she noticed how the corners of his lips turned up slightly. She turned and walked along to her bedroom. As soon as she was inside she locked the door and crossed to the bed.

She was more frightened than she had ever before been: even more frightened than the time fifteen years ago when a policeman had come to tell her about her late husband's crash and she had guessed what he was going to say because of the look on his face. Now she was terrified only for the girl. Her own body had ceased to mean much and had Krammer been threatening her she would not have been terrified, only fearful: but that girl, with naturally blonde hair, a gamin attractiveness, the glorious zest of youth, was in such revolting danger that it frightened her to think about it.

She had to get help.

Krammer had looked worn out. As soon as he lay down on a bed he would fall asleep and must surely sleep very deeply. That meant she must wait as long as possible before creeping downstairs to telephone the police. If she spoke quietly into the receiver there was no chance he would hear her. If the police surrounded the house and moved really quickly they'd be able to catch him in time.

She tried to imagine how any man could be such a sadist

as Krammer was and then, inevitably, began to wonder if this soft-spoken, well-mannered man was really the monster he was supposed to be? He must have killed those girls, because he had been found guilty at his trial, but was it even conceivable that he had known what he was doing? Surely, now, he must have recovered considerably to be able to behave so rationally and courteously? Yet if that were true, why had he brought the girl here? What was he going to do to her?

She stood up, crossed to the mantelpiece over the fire, and stared at the studio photograph of her husband. She must call the police: she must save the girl. Sarah was the daughter she had so passionately wanted. If she had had a child the death of her late husband would not have been quite such a paralysing blow: she would have been forced to consider someone other than herself.

She looked at her gold wristwatch. Only ten minutes had passed since she had come into her bedroom. She raised the watch to her ears and listened to see if it had stopped, but it was ticking as regularly as ever. She picked up a woollen dressing-gown and put it on.

If only Krammer had not said that the name Amelia reminded him of flowering cherries in spring: her late husband had said something very much like that to her. The exact words escaped her, as so much of her married life now escaped her through becoming hidden behind the haze of fifteen years. Fifteen years ago she had been certain she would remember everything for always, but she didn't.

She looked at the time again. Only another five minutes had gone by. How long must she wait before she went downstairs to the telephone? Half an hour? An hour? The longer the better, except that she seemed to have read somewhere that the deepest sleep came at the beginning? She wondered if Krammer slept as soundly as her late husband had done? She had always laughed and said that the hounds of hell wouldn't have awoken him. The hounds of hell must bay often around Krammer.

Thirty minutes gone. What had the parents been doing to let the girl be on her own in the middle of the night? One couldn't pick up a paper, listen to the wireless, or watch the television, without being warned that he had escaped from prison, that he was still free, and that he was a desperately dangerous man. Hadn't the parents ever had enough love for their daughter to guard her against a man like Krammer? Why did those who longed for children so often never have them, and those who didn't care or didn't want them so often produce them by the score?

Forty-five minutes. She daren't switch on any of the stair or hall lights, or use a torch. He might have left the door of his bedroom open. But darkness wouldn't hinder her, because she knew every inch of the house. She would avoid the door-stops, the worn patches in the stair carpet, the creaking fourth stair from the bottom, and the large Chinese jar which had been given to them by her late husband's mother.

Sixty minutes. She kicked off her sheepskin mules and walked over to the door, where she switched off the main light. She waited in the darkness, listening, and the only sounds she could hear were those of a heavy lorry driving quickly along the main road.

She opened the door, very slowly because it creaked. Twice it tried to make a noise, but she was able to stop it. When sufficiently open, she stepped out into the corridor.

The ticking of the grandmother clock seemed to her to become louder and louder. She held out her right hand at shoulder level and moved right until her fingers touched the wall. She walked to the head of the stairs, silently praying that Krammer would go on sleeping.

The stairs carpet was only badly worn on the half-landing, but she took the greatest possible care to make certain her bare feet were not caught up in any other stray threads. The banisters were creaky so she kept on the wall side. She stepped from the fifth stair down to the third, having counted her way from the half-landing.

Krammer hadn't come out of his bedroom. She only needed a few more seconds to reach the telephone, then she could dial O. It was still a manual exchange so that O had to do for the emergency call as well as for the normal call to the exchange.

She reached the telephone and lifted the receiver, dialled O. At that moment the hall light was switched on and Krammer moved quickly forward from the doorway of the sitting-room. He reached out for the receiver and she struggled to keep hold of it. 'Help,' she shouted wildly, 'Stoneyacre three eight three.'

He used all of his extraordinary strength to overcome her resistance and force her to drop the receiver. It fell the length of the cord and then swung a few inches above the ground. Krammer twisted her wrist violently and she was thrown sideways against the wall, from which she fell down to the ground. He picked up the receiver and replaced it.

'I came downstairs when you went into your bedroom in case you tried this,' he said simply. 'Do you really want me to kill her?'

'No, please no. You musn't,' she answered desperately.

'But if the police come here I shall have to kill her. Can't you understand that?'

Her dressing-gown and nightdress had, because of her fall, ridden up over her knees. She pulled them down and then slowly came to her feet. Her wrist was aching badly and she dully wondered if it had been sprained.

'You could so easily have made me kill her,' he said.

'Why won't you let her go?' she asked shrilly.

'I can't. But you musn't do anything to make me kill her: you must help me. Let's go upstairs now and then I'll lock you in your bedroom just to make sure. You won't do anything more like trying to escape, will you? I'm sure you wouldn't want to be responsible for her death. Did you ever have a daughter?'

'No.'

'Wouldn't you have liked to have a daughter like her?'

'Please . . .'

'Then remember how much it would hurt you to know you had helped to kill her. Shall we go back upstairs now?'

She returned to the stairs and began to climb them. As she stepped on to the fourth one, it creaked loudly.

.   .   .   .   .

At Stoneyacre telephone exchange a yawning operator stirred his tea and then drank it. Some people were so bloody impatient, it wasn't true. Just because their call didn't get answered at the first ring they packed it in. At this time of the morning did they expect instant service?

Nine

The search began at daybreak and the control van was parked on the London road in the middle of Stoneyacre Common. The dog handlers and uniformed men were called to the van and briefed by the assistant chief constable who had taken over direct command of the operation. There were twelve dog handlers, the maximum number that experience showed could be worked together, and about fifty constables and sergeants. Three dog handlers and eight constables were issued with R/T sets and given individual call signs. Everyone was shown first the large-scale, twenty-five inches to the mile, map of the area and then the master control plan with the common squared off to show the boxes that were to be searched in strict order.

After the briefing the men moved to the far end of the common, where they lined up along the road, with never more than a hundred yards between dogs. Behind them was the inspector in charge of the dog handlers and the superintendent in charge of field operations.

The search began. Orders, both verbal and through R/T, kept the line reasonably straight and the men moved slowly, using sticks to part the long grass or bushes, whilst the dogs quartered the ground.

A whole host of objects were found, clearly none of which had any connexion with Sarah Bramswell, but were the rubbish of a consumer society. The end of the common was reached and the men moved along, re-formed, and came back over fresh ground. The dogs, Alsatians except for one Dobermann, worked steadily on, noses scenting both the ground and the air. They could keep going for a maximum of four hours before fresh dogs would have to be brought in to the line.

In the control van the assistant chief constable stared at one of the large-scale maps as he tried to check with himself that everything possible was being done or would very soon be done. Within half an hour two hundred policemen would be brought to the area to spread the search into the surrounding countryside; a team of twenty-five detectives would begin questioning every nearby house-holder, breaking into Sunday morning sleep, asking whether he or she had heard or seen anything the previous night; two helicopters were being called up for an aerial search; a road block was already set up on the London road, not far away, and every motorist was to be asked if he had been on the road during the previous night and whether he had seen or heard anything; appeals were to be made by car loudhailers, on the wireless and the TV, for any information which could possibly help; another appeal would be made for civilian searchers which must result in thousands coming forward. . . . What else could possibly be done to try to find the girl?

.   .   .   .   .

Agar stopped at his house at 6.30 when the sun was already fairly high and the air was warm. As he shut the front door and walked towards the kitchen Caroline appeared at the head of the stairs and looked down at him.

'Have you found her?' she asked.

'No.'

'Oh, Bill. I haven't been able to sleep properly. I've been lying in the dark, thinking how I'd be feeling if it was my daughter who was missing and I've been praying you'd find her, safe.'

'I know.'

She came down the stairs. He put his arm round her waist and for a few seconds sought the comfort of feeling her against himself, knowing that she was safe and sound. 'I saw the parents, Carry.'

'How . . . how were they?'

'Terrified, desperate, sick with fear, hoping for a miracle even though they're almost certain that one's impossible.' He let go of her. 'I'm going to rustle up a very quick breakfast before I move on to H.Q.'

'I'll do it for you, Bill.'

They went through to the kitchen. He noticed, with the heightened perception that so often came to him at times of crisis, that the wall paint was badly blistered in several places and the ancient cooker looked to be on its last legs.

'Eggs and bacon, Bill?' she asked.

'And fried bread and anything else lying about in the larder. I could eat an elephant.' He sat down at the table and yawned three times.

She put the frying-pan on the cooker and lit the gas. 'What's happening now, Bill?' she asked.

'They're searching the common first and then spreading out in concentric circles. Later on today everybody south of the Thames is going to be asked to search his land, or if there's too much of it for him then to contact his local police. As it's a Sunday, churches will be in use, but that leaves factories, warehouses, and so on, where he might be hiding up. We're asking owners, managers, foremen, anyone available, to search every factory or other building normally empty on Sundays. We're requesting the public to give every ounce of help they can, and they will. This will be one of those times when the police and the public really work together all the way.'

She cut the rind off three rashers of bacon and put the bacon into the frying-pan. 'If he's got her, Bill, how long will it be before . . .'

'Before he starts torturing her? God knows. All we can say is that those other poor little kids were alive for about four days before he finally killed them.'

'It's like Auschwitz.'

He ate quickly when the meal was ready, drinking three cups of coffee during it. Then he went upstairs and shaved, nicking his chin because the head of his electric razor was damaged. After that he left the house and drove across town to H.Q.

His room at H.Q. was empty, but on his desk was a Telex message. He picked up the strip of paper, Sellotaped up the centre where it had been torn when removed carelessly from the machine, and read the message, whose origin was J.A.P. Section 9. A footprint had been found not far from the potting shed in the garden in Surrey and it was now certain that no one in the house had made it. It was formed by a boot size nine and a half, which had a composition sole and a rubber heel: the rubber heel, pattern M72, was worn on the right-hand side (area about five square centimetres). Krammer was believed to wear a boot size between nine and ten inclusive. Boots with composition soles and rubber heels, pattern M72, were worn by prisoners at Lettsworth Prison: other patterns were also in use and there could be no final certainty of the origin of this print.

Agar left his room and went up the main staircase to the Operations Room, at the far end of which was Records. Clanton, who was standing in front of the wall-size map of the county in which coloured lights denoted the last known positions of police cars and wireless-equipped motor-cycles, asked him if he'd seen the message on his desk. After replying that he had, Agar walked through to the first of the three far rooms. A uniformed sergeant stood up and Agar asked for Boots and Shoes. After a very brief search in a filing cabinet the sergeant handed him a thin, green covered book in which were photographs of forty-five sole patterns and one hundred and sixty-two heel patterns. M72 was an ordinary, six circle, outer raised rib pattern, with the raised manufacturer's trade mark to the rear. He copied the pattern into his notebook.

After he had handed the reference list back to the sergeant Agar leaned against the table and lit a cigarette. So far, all they knew was that probably Krammer had been in that potting shed. A goddamn' lot of use that knowledge was to Sarah Bramswell. . . .

He jerked himself upright and walked back through Operations to the main staircase. Leaning against a table, worrying himself sick, wasn't going to help anyone.

* * * * *

It was 6.30 a.m.

Mrs. Pretty looked at her face in the gilt framed mirror over the fireplace. Under her over-large eyes were the ugly shadowy semicircles of sleeplessness, her hair was in lifeless disarray, and there was an ugly bruise on the side of her neck.

Why couldn't she think what to do? she asked herself desperately. She wasn't afraid of Krammer. If any action by her could be successful she wouldn't refrain from it because it might result in physical hurt to herself. But her mind seemed to have been anaesthetized by her fear for the girl. By a cruel mental transference she felt that it was her own daughter who was in such terrible danger and he had told her that if he discovered her once more trying to call in help he would kill Sarah. He had been all too explicit on that point. She believed his threat. As he had said, he had absolutely nothing to lose if he did kill Sarah: he couldn't lay himself open to any greater punishment than he had already received. He had told her exactly how he would kill Sarah and the description had made her feel sick.

How was she going to get a message for help through without Krammer's knowing it? There was the telephone, but her previous attempt to use it had ended in abject failure. A second failure—so easily brought about—would mean that he would go straight up to that bedroom and murder Sarah. Could she overcome Krammer? Common sense told her there was no hope of that. For a woman she was reasonably strong, but he had the strength of a . . . a madman. What about drink? Perhaps. A weapon? He had her revolver and the only other possibility was a large knife, like a carving knife.

There must be some trick by which she could get the better of him. Then, as she tried to think of one, her mind was flooded once more by fear for Sarah.

She suddenly remembered the postman. She received letters from her late husband's friend who managed her financial affairs, her bank, begging societies, and occasionally various members of her late husband's family when they thought they ought to do their duty. If this were one of the days when the postman called she might get a chance to speak to him. If she met him at the door and Krammer was not around it would be all right. But she had to know Krammer was not around because if she made a mistake and he heard her, he would go up those stairs, into Sarah's room, and . . .

The postman came somewhere between 7.15 and 7.30 except when the snow was thick, the pools forms arrived for everyone in the area, the electricity bills were sent out, or around Christmas.

It was now 6.48.

She dressed, combed her hair, and went to the door. It was locked from the outside. She turned round and looked at the window. He had screwed it up last night and then gone on to say that even if she somehow managed to open it and escape, neither she nor anyone else could get back in without his knowing about it.

She banged on the door and continued until the key was turned. Then she opened the door and went into the passage, dark and sombre because age had blackened the wallpaper and ceiling. He stood and looked at her in his quiet, vaguely enquiring way, only his pale blue eyes showing any real animation.

'I want to go to the bathroom.' She spoke far more loudly than she had intended.

'I'm so sorry,' he replied, as if he really meant it.

'Is Sarah all right?'

'She's still fast asleep. I looked into her room just a minute ago and she was sleeping with her hair spread all round her face so that she looked just like an angel.'

The use of such a word shocked her, but she wasn't certain why. Perhaps, she thought, it was because she had always imagined that someone as bestial as Krammer could never believe in angels. 'I want to see her,' she said.

He looked a little doubtful.

'She must be horribly scared. If I see her I may be able to help her be not quite so scared.'

'I don't think we ought to risk waking her after the long night she had. Perhaps later on.'

She went past him and along to the end of the corridor to the bathroom and lavatory.

It was 7.05 when she left the bathroom. Krammer was not in the corridor. She made her way downstairs and into the sitting-room. It was in its usual untidy state. Magazines lay open on the floor, some knitting and the concomitant ball of wool were in the middle of the settee, the *Radio Times* had dropped behind the TV set, two old newspapers had fallen out of the waste-paper basket and on the pouf, which she and her late husband had bought on their round-the-world honeymoon, was the tray on which were the remains of her supper of the previous night. She ignored the mess and crossed to the nearer bay window from which she could clearly see the front drive.

As she watched the drive she listened to every sound that reached her from within the house. Had Krammer remained upstairs? What was she going to say to the postman? The police must realize that they had to move so quickly and quietly that Krammer never had a chance to kill the girl. He must be got downstairs and held down there by every means at her disposal.

She looked at her watch. Seven-twenty. Wasn't the postman coming? Surely Fate wouldn't be so cruel as to make this a letterless day. Someone must have written to her. She felt queasy, as she had always done when waiting for something important to happen. The day of her marriage she had almost been sick.

Seven-thirty-five and no postman. He could be late, for once. Perhaps there was some publicity campaign with hundreds of advertisements being sent through the post so that the postmen delivering had had to visit every house in the area.

Then she remembered it was Sunday.

Ten

Mrs. Pretty stared round the sitting-room and looked again at the dishevelled state it was in, but her mind recorded nothing of this. It was Sunday morning and Fate had been cruel enough to make this a letterless day.

Automatically, because it was something she had done so often since Krammer had broken into the house, she looked at her watch. Seven-forty-two. She felt so defeated that it seemed there could be no point in fighting on. Then, by a supreme effort of will, she forced herself to look forward in time, not back. If there was no post there must be something else. She remembered the Sunday newspapers, delivered by a boy of about fourteen who rode a brilliantly painted bicycle and who whistled hopelessly out of tune. But he would be unable to help. He was too young for her to take the risk that he might not act exactly as she told him to, but in any case he left the papers in the little box at the end of the drive in which she had put a two-shilling piece the previous afternoon.

Slowly she walked out of the sitting-room into the hall and as she stood there she became aware of movement upstairs. She looked up. Krammer was standing at the head of the stairs. He had changed out of the uniform into a light grey suit that fitted him remarkably well.

She shuddered. 'Oh God, no!' she muttered brokenly.

He had heard what she said. He gestured vaguely with his left hand. 'What's wrong, Amelia?'

'That suit.'

He looked down at it, then back at her. 'I found it in a cupboard with several other suits. I didn't think you'd really mind if I borrowed it. Do you mind?'

She didn't want to explain, but it was almost as if she spoke the words despite herself. 'My late husband was the last person to wear it and . . . and just for a second you looked a bit like him.'

'I'm terribly sorry.'

'It doesn't matter,' she said flatly.

He walked down the stairs, moving all the time with great precision as if he thought about each step before he took it. When he reached the floor he spoke. 'Sarah's woken up and she says she's quite hungry. She wonders if she could have an egg, boiled for four minutes. She doesn't like them when they get hard and she just can't stand them when they're so soft they're runny. Her mother always boils them for exactly four minutes. I hope you've got some eggs?'

'Yes.'

'And if you've any brown bread she prefers that to white: especially the kind that's all nutty.'

'There's only white.'

'I'm sure she won't mind.'

'I'll go through to the kitchen. When it's ready I'll take the tray up to her.'

'I'm sorry, Amelia, but I'd much rather you didn't, I really would.'

'Why?'

'Please don't ask me that just now. You won't be too long, will you? She's so hungry.'

   •   •   •   •   •

7.53 a.m. The sun was high now and the shadows were appreciably shortening and moving round to the north: the day was going to be a real scorcher. Swallows performed the most amazing aerial acrobatics and far beyond them a massive airliner sedately lumbered across the sky in a straight line, leaving behind it four vapour trails which merged immediately into two and then a little further back into one.

The searching policemen were already sweating and most of them had taken off their jackets. The dogs were panting, but the pace at which they quartered the ground had barely diminished and they 'spoke' with undiminished keenness whenever they scented any foreign object: a quick nervous tension gripped every man who heard the barking, because this might be what they were looking for, but each time the report went along the line by R/T and word of mouth that it was another false alarm.

Then, at 7.59, it was no longer a false alarm, although it was very nearly dismissed as such.

A black and tan Alsatian barked and the long line of men came to a halt. They were almost up to the road on a return sweep and ahead of them was a slight slope up to the narrow pavement. The dog's handler went forward and saw that the dog was indicating a roll of binder twine that was brand new. He spoke to the next man. 'Nothing.'

'Again? What's up? Your mongrel gone soft in the head and taken up barking at shadows?'

The handler, his quick temper in evidence, called the constable a lot of Anglo-Saxon words and then said that his dog was telling him there was a ball of binder twine in the stinging nettles—but only a fool would suggest the twine could have anything to do with the kid. The constable, sufficiently far away from any superiors to have loosened his tie and undone his collar, walked forward and stared at the twine. 'D'you know how much that lot cost?'

'No.'

'Enough to make me certain we'd better tell the brass hats or they'll take us apart.' The constable called across to the nearest man, sweating heartily, who was carrying an R/T set. 'Fred, tell 'em we've got a brand-new ball of binder twine here.'

The message was passed back to the field officers and the control van. The control van ordered the line to stay halted and the handler and dog to move back from the site. There was a pause of about a minute and then a black Austin came to a tyre-squealing halt on the road and Detective Superintendent Pearce and Detective Inspector Raydon climbed out of it.

The two detectives slowly walked down the sloping bank, visually examining every inch of ground before stepping on it. They came to the patch of stinging nettles and the ball of twine. Both their minds had the same thought. It was a very odd thing for anyone to throw away or lose: one didn't easily lose a ball of twine about six inches high and nine inches in diameter, weighing several pounds. Yet surely it was a remote possibility that this could have anything to do with the missing girl? They continued to stare at the twine as if by doing so it might answer them.

Back on the road, Agar braked his Morris to a halt behind the Austin and climbed out. He crossed the pavement and stood at the top of the shallow slope. 'What's up, sir?'

Pearce spoke without bothering to turn round. 'You tell us.'

Raydon answered the question. 'A ball of twine, Bill, brand new. So what's it doing here?'

Agar began to walk down the slope on a different approach from the one the other two detectives had taken: like them, he visually searched the ground to make certain he disturbed nothing of importance and that was how he saw the footprint.

He knelt down. There was a patch of earth where the grass had been killed at some time and the top-soil had dried out so finely that it had almost the composition of sand. The heel of a shoe had pressed down here and left an imprint which was just discernible.

'Found something, Agar?' demanded the detective superintendent.

'Footprint,' he replied, his voice slightly muffled because of the position he was in.

'Good God, man, there must be a million and one footprints on this common! We'd better get the line started again. I'll take the twine back to the van, but it doesn't look at all warm to me.'

'Just hold it a minute, will you, sir?' Agar took his notebook from his pocket and tore out a sheet which he held at the back of the print to see if it would reflect light and help him to distinguish the pattern. It didn't. He cursed the dry dust which so tantalizingly only half offered a pattern. He wondered whether he dared damp it and decided against this.

The other two detectives came and stood and watched him. He moved round on his knees until he was at ninety degrees to his previous position, and now, by letting his cheek lie on the grass and holding the paper at forty-five degrees, he could make out the pattern sufficiently clearly to be certain what it was. He sat up, opened his notebook at the first page and studied the sketch he had made of print pattern M72. It matched the one in the dust: also the latter had a blank right-hand corner where the pattern on the heel had been worn away.

'Well?' snapped Pearce impatiently, 'is this a solo prayer session or can we all join in?'

Agar stood up and dusted his knees. 'There was a message at H.Q. early this morning, sir, from Section 9, J.A.P. They found a footprint by that potting shed Krammer probably slept in. I can be ninety-five per cent certain that that heelmark is the same as the one here.'

The superintendent dropped down on to his knees and studied the print, much as Agar had done, first from one side and then from the other.

He stood up. 'Let's see your sketch.' When Agar gave him the notebook, opened at the first page, he stared at the sketch for a long time. Then he handed the notebook back. 'They match.' He shoved his hands into his pockets and his big frame seemed to droop, as if he were relaxing every muscle. 'Clear a circle round here for fifty yards and bring in three men to carry out a blade by blade search of the grass. The rest of the line form up for the next beat.'

Orders were given and men and dogs took up their new positions. Three constables who remained behind were told to start an intensive search of the fifty-yard circle. Agar, who was holding the ball of twine, twisted it round and upside down without finding anything of interest about it.

A large black Humber drew up behind the other two cars and the assistant chief constable climbed out of the back. He called the detective superintendent across and listened to the latter's report, then asked for, and was given, the ball of twine. He was about to say something when he was interrupted.

'Sir,' called out one of the three constables.

They all turned. 'What?' shouted Pearce.

'There's something here, sir. Looks like blood.'

They went down the slope and stopped where the constable was pointing. Here, over an area of about a square foot, there were dull, rust-coloured stains on the grass.

Raydon called across to a waiting R/T man and gave

orders for a message to be sent back to the control van asking for scissors, plastic bags, and a cameraman.

Agar left the others and returned to the road. Standing clear of the gutter, which would now be minutely searched, he lit a cigarette. Was it the girl's blood or Krammer's? If the girl had had the chance to fight she might have managed to scratch or bite him severely. How did the blood come to be at the bottom of the slope? Did the binder twine have any bearing on the case? A number of questions without answers, yet one thing was now near enough certain to be taken as such—it had been Krammer who was responsible for Sarah Bramswell's disappearance.

He looked along the road and saw a uniformed constable and a man in plain clothes hurrying along towards where he stood. Beyond them were the two police vans and then came the inevitable onlookers, held back by the police, watching with ghoulish pleasure.

The constable had brought plastic bags and a pair of scissors, the detective a camera. Pearce, after replacing the ball of twine in the stinging nettles, waited until several photographs had been taken and then he cut the grass himself and put it into three plastic bags. He picked up the ball of twine once more and handed it to Raydon. 'We'll assume this has some bearing.'

Finally a police car was called up and the bags of grass and the twine were given to the driver, who was ordered to get them to the laboratories at Scotland Yard so damn' quickly he took all the treads off the tyres.

.   .   .   .   .

Mrs. Pretty washed up the breakfast things, using soap powder because she refused to believe detergents were nearly as efficient. She deliberately attempted to live in the past, treasuring all the old things and certain nothing new was any good. For her the date of her late husband's death marked a point beyond which everything was new.

She put the plates in the rack. Sarah had eaten all her breakfast except for half a slice of bread and butter. That, at least, was cheering. A child who ate well was a child who was still fit.

She had to do something to save the girl. That thought kept filling her mind. She must do something, instead of remaining passive. But what could she do that might offer any hope? The most frightening thing was the slender thread on which Sarah's life hung. Let Krammer interrupt any attempt of hers to call for help and he would kill the girl immediately: such death would mean nothing to him. Then she had the terrible thought that perhaps her duty was to precipitate a crisis because even if Krammer carried out his bestial threat it would be far, far better for the girl than to suffer the unspeakable agonies that those other girls had suffered. Sarah would know only minutes of hell, not days. But could she, Amelia Pretty, retain her sanity if she knew she had been so directly responsible for the girl's murder? Wasn't there so much truth in the saying that where there was life there was hope?

She wildly remembered the old, old problem. If a mother and her child were drowning, and only one of them could be saved, which one should it be?

Krammer entered the kitchen. 'It's such a lovely hot day. It makes me want to go on a picnic.'

She began to dry the plates, cups, and saucers that were in the broken-down rack—like so much in the house, it needed renewing—with a rose-patterned teacloth.

'Let me do that,' he said suddenly, and he took the cloth from her. 'D'you know, Amelia, I used to go for picnics in the hills. Up in Cumberland, that is, where I was born.'

'Yes.'

'You knew that? But, of course, you read about me in the papers. You've got to understand something. They told lies and they didn't understand. I did hurt some cats, but it wasn't like the papers said and it didn't give me a sadistic pleasure: that man Todd told me it was clever to do that sort of thing and I so wanted to be clever. Do you think you can understand that?'

'Yes,' she answered, without meaning it. She could not comprehend that any reason for burning cats to death could appear adequate to a young boy.

Apparently unaware of the direction her thoughts had taken, he went on speaking. 'Of course, they weren't proper picnics.' He carefully put a newly dried plate on the central wooden table which was covered with some torn oil-cloth. 'I hadn't any money then. But I used to take a slice of bread from the kitchen and sometimes I'd put on it some jam or dripping, if I could find any, and I'd leave home and climb up the sheep paths to the tops of the hills at the back of the house. I used to sit up there and imagine I was a god. I could look all round and not see another person and it's the only time in my life I've felt really free.'

She turned round quickly and was careless that she was holding the worn mop so that it dripped on to the floor. 'You've just said how you liked to be free on a mountain top. Can't you understand, then, how she wants to be free? You must understand that.'

'I know it.'

'Then why won't you let her go?'

'I can't, not just yet.'

'When will you?'

'After four days.'

'God, no!' she cried. 'Not that. You can't do that.'

He carefully dried the last plate. 'I promise you there's

nothing to get worried about.' He touched her right arm, just below the rolled-up blouse she was wearing.

She jerked her arm free and stared wildly at a knife which lay on the table.

He followed her gaze and saw the knife. He seemed to sigh before he moved, as precisely as ever, to the table and picked up the knife, which, over the years, had worn until it had a sharp pointed blade six inches long. He drove the blade through the oil-cloth into the table and then wrenched it sideways so that it snapped just below the handle. 'There are still two cups to wash up,' he said. 'Shall we do them?' He dropped the handle on to the table.

Dully, she looked for the cups and then saw them at the far end of the wooden draining-board. As she washed them she wondered bitterly if she would ever have found the courage to use that knife.

'I was talking to Sarah about a picnic while she ate her breakfast,' he said reminiscently. 'She's a wonderful little girl and so intelligent. She told me how she and her mother and father go down to the seaside and picnic on the beach. She says she loves the sea when the waves are big and break with a roar and a hiss because it shows what power the sea has. I don't suppose many girls of her age would have the intelligence to think like that, do you?'

'I've no idea.'

'You told me you didn't ever have any children, didn't you, Amelia?'

'Yes.'

'Did you want them? I mean, would you have liked to have children?'

She washed the last cup and pulled the plug out of the sink. The water drained away with noisy gurgling.

'Would you?'

'Yes,' she answered, in almost a whisper.

'I'm so glad. I knew you were that kind of a person. Before I forget it, Amelia, I asked Sarah what she would like for lunch and she said her favourite food is tinned salmon with lots of vinegar. I wonder if you've got any tinned salmon?'

'Yes.'

'That's wonderful, because she'll be so delighted. She told me she's only allowed to have it on special occasions because her mother says that if she has it often she won't keep on finding it a treat. Her mother must be a very sensible person, mustn't she, and really love her daughter?'

Mrs. Pretty made some comment and seconds later could not have said what it was. Quite suddenly she had thought of how to give the alarm without his being able to know anything about it. On the eight o'clock news there had been a long police message saying that Sarah Bramswell was missing and there was reason for believing Krammer was responsible for her disappearance. Because of this, people were asked to report anything unusual that happened, no matter how silly or trivial the unusual thing might seem to be or how many false alarms this caused. Such a police request must alert everyone. Therefore she would telephone the local shops to give her weekly orders, but she would give orders that must make them realize something was wrong. Then, as she was deciding what to ask for that would inevitably cause comment she remembered once again it was Sunday. Krammer would know that no one ever normally telephoned orders to shops on a Sunday, even in the country.

'Were you going to say something?' he asked. 'You looked as if you were.'

She was about to deny it when one more possibility came to mind. In a fraction of time she had worked out what she was going to do. 'I always go to church on Sundays.'

He carefully placed the drying-up cloth on a wooden rail and arranged it so that it would dry properly. 'I'm afraid you can't go today: it just isn't possible.'

'But I promise not to say anything.'

He shook his head. 'It wouldn't be fair to put you to such temptation.'

'I always arrange the flowers after communion and before the morning service.'

'I'm sure they'll find someone else. In prison there was always someone to do that sort of thing.'

'If I can't go I must tell them I shan't be doing the flowers so they can try to get someone else. I must telephone the vicar.'

He thought about it. 'I suppose that's right. It's so lovely to see nice flowers in church. Now, shall we put all this crockery away? Then I must go on up and see how Sarah is and whether there's anything she wants. Suppose she would like some milk, have you got plenty?'

'Not very much.'

'Then you'd better ask for a little more. You write the note to the milkman and I'll put it out. Where does he leave it?'

'Outside the pantry.'

'Is that the pantry through there? Ask for two pints, will you? Even if Sarah wants plenty that should be enough because I only have milk in coffee and never in tea.'

She opened the right-hand top drawer of the old Welsh dresser and brought out a notebook. She wrote *Two pints please* on the top page, tore it out, and gave it to him. He read it, twice, and turned the page over to make certain nothing was written there. Then they walked through the pantry, which she used as a storeroom, and he unbolted and opened the outside door. She looked past his shoulder at the large circular rose bed.

'Whereabouts shall we leave this message?'

'On that box.'

He read the message through once more and placed the paper under a stone which lay on top of the wooden box. They returned inside the house and he locked the door and bolted it.

She led the way through the kitchen into the hall and went over to the telephone. She picked up the directory and searched through the Rs until she found Roydon, The Rev. J. She dialled the number. As she listened to the ringing note, she watched Krammer walk slowly round the hall, examining the three oil paintings with the air of someone who really appreciated art. She had the strange impression that he was trying not to embarrass her too much while listening to what she said.

Abruptly, the ringing stopped and a woman's voice said: 'This is Stoneyacre three double two.'

'Mrs. Roydon?' She tried desperately to keep any suspicion of excitement out of her voice.

'Yes.'

'It's Amelia Pretty here. I've rung to say I'm terribly sorry, but I'm not feeling very well and I shan't be able to arrange the flowers in church this morning.'

'I beg your pardon?'

'You will be able to get someone else, won't you? I'm sure someone else will have a few flowers in the garden to spare. It's such a pity I can't make it.'

'But, Mrs. Pretty, I'm very sorry I don't understand what you're talking about. John hasn't said anything to me about your arranging flowers. In fact, I'm almost certain that Mrs. Avory——'

'I know, it'll be the first time I've missed a Sunday since you and your husband came to this parish. Still, with any luck I shall be all right by next week. Good-bye, Mrs. Roydon.' She replaced the receiver.

Krammer spoke. 'I'm sure they'll be able to get someone else to do the flowers.'

The vicar's wife must realize what that call meant, thought Mrs. Pretty. In the five years that the Roydons had held the living of Stoneyacre she had not set foot inside the church. All she did was to send a cheque for five guineas every Easter. Mrs. Roydon must realize what that call really meant.

.   .   .   .   .

At the vicarage Mrs. Roydon heard her husband come down the stairs. 'John,' she called out.

He came into the study. 'What is it, dear? I must get to the church or I shall be late.'

'Mrs. Pretty has just rung me.'

'A very mixed honour, I feel.'

'She apologized for not being able to come to church to arrange the flowers and does hope you'll be able to find someone else.'

'She what?'

'That's what she said.'

'Potty, completely potty. I've always said a person can't divorce herself from the world and remain sane and normal. Now I must get over to the church before the choir begins to asssemble.'

Eleven

Throughout the Sunday morning, police appeals to the public continued to be made and the response was heartening. Volunteers by the hundred arrived in Stoneyacre by every possible means of transport and it needed sixty policemen merely to organize them.

Scotland Yard had been called in by the chief constable, and a team, headed by a commander, arrived at 11.05. For once their appearance caused no resentment amongst the county police: the devil himself would have been welcomed, could he have helped.

Sweating men leaned over large-scale maps of the countryside, boxing it as earlier they had boxed Stoneyacre Common and the land immediately around it. Parties of searchers, a hundred strong, were sent to cover each box and with most of them went a dog and handler, these teams having been called in from all parts of the Home Counties. Another two helicopters were brought into service. A continuous road watch was maintained throughout the county by hundreds of volunteer drivers who covered all the roads as they looked for anything suspicious. All these activities caused misunderstanding, lost tempers, accidents, and even injuries, but nothing halted the search. For tens of miles around Stoneyacre the telephone calls to the police became so numerous that switchboards were swamped. Police were drafted into the area and when there were no more men available in the county the chief constables of other counties immediately responded to the request for help. The army was asked to set up alternative and supplementary lines of communication.

The sun reached its zenith and poured its heat over a countryside in which men and women gave up their free Sunday to help try to find the twelve-year-old girl who was missing.

Slowly the sun arched downwards and the shadows lengthened and moved eastward.

Every hour that went by without success meant one more hour during which Sarah Bramswell would be suffering in a way that people tried not to think about. No one knew how soon Krammer had begun to assault and torture those other girls: it was just known that after about four days they finally and mercifully died. Sarah Bramswell had now been missing for fifteen hours.

Agar was in the operations van, talking by telephone—recently connected to the overhead wires by G.P.O. engineers —to his opposite number in J.A.P., Section 9, when one of the other two telephones on the small table rang. The sergeant answered it and then hurriedly wrote something in a note-book. As soon as he had finished his conversation Agar leaned over to see what the sergeant had written and he saw the two letters 'AB'. It was obvious this was the blood group to which the dried blood on the grass belonged. Seconds later the sergeant terminated the conversation and replaced the receiver. He looked up. 'The lab., sir, with the blood on the grass.'

'I'll tell them outside.'

'Very good, sir.'

Agar squeezed past the sergeant and went out on to the road. The senior police officers were in a group, studying a map which had been draped over the bonnet of a car and which had to be held down against the light breeze. He went up to the car and after a while Detective Superintendent Pearce turned round. Pearce's face was flushed, showing he had been arguing.

'Blood group's through from the lab., sir. AB.'

The other men had become silent as soon as he spoke and his words were interrupted only by the flapping sound of the map against the car's bonnet.

'Isn't AB the rarest group?' asked the assistant chief constable.

'Yes, sir,' replied Agar. 'Five per cent of the population or thereabouts.'

'Does anyone know the girl's group?'

There was no answer.

'Why the devil hasn't that been done?'

Once again there was silence.

'Agar,' snapped Pearce, 'find out the girl's group and Krammer's.'

Agar left and returned to his Morris, looking scruffy amongst the senior police officers' cars. He drove towards the centre of Stoneyacre. At the end of the common a uniformed policeman was on point duty, keeping the traffic moving and the crowds back. A television interviewer tried to question Agar, as he stopped the car to the constable's signal, and thrust a microphone through the open window. Agar refused to answer and when the constable waved him on he drove on careless about the interviewer. This might be news, but it was also a human tragedy and he did not believe human tragedies should be fed to the millions.

He reached Bramswell's house. It looked very drab in the strong sunshine, with peeling paintwork and badly stained and faded colour-washed walls. He parked his car and pushed his way through the throng of sightseers. From behind him there came a rising hubbub as the people discussed his visit.

The front door was opened by a woman he had never seen before. After he had introduced himself she told him she was Betty's sister. Betty was ill in bed and under sedation. Her husband was in the dining-room. She let him into the house and then took him into the dining-room. Charles Bramswell sat at the far end of the table, a glass of whisky in one hand, a cigarette in the other. He had not shaved or washed. In the short time since Agar had last seen him he appeared to have aged several years.

Bramswell looked up and he squinted slightly, as if having trouble in focussing his eyes. 'Have you found anything?'

'I'm terribly sorry, no.'

'Christ!' he groaned. He drank the whisky and poured himself another from the three-parts-empty bottle. He added very little water. 'D'you want to hear something? I've been praying she's already dead, that's what I've been doing. I love her, as much as Betty. But I've been wishing her dead. That's odd, isn't it? That's so bloody odd, I want to . . .' He drank, drew on the cigarette, and then stubbed it out. 'My wife cursed me just before she got too sleepy to curse anyone. She cursed me for going to the meeting of the Moral Action Group. If I hadn't gone I could have driven Sarah back home. But how could I have known that? For God's sake tell me, how? I didn't know; I just didn't know. Can you feel what it's like, sitting here, thinking?'

'I can imagine,' said Agar.

'When have you ever had a daughter picked up by a sex maniac who's murdered God knows how many kids of her age? When have you sat at a table, drinking whisky to drown your thoughts? And only making yourself think all the harder? You've no idea of the agony. I'll tell you, I wept just now: wept as I haven't done since I was a little snot-nosed kid, thirty-five years ago.' He drank again. 'So what does that make me? Weak?'

'Just someone suffering most terribly.'

It was not the answer Bramswell had expected. He was silent for a long time, then he looked at the other as he pushed the bottle of whisky across the table. Agar shook his head.

'D'you want something?' asked Bramswell, in a voice suddenly dead.

'Can you tell me what blood group your daughter is?'

Frowning slightly, he looked at Agar. 'Why d'you want to know that?'

Agar answered directly. 'There was some blood on the grass at a point of the common where we think Krammer met your daughter.'

'Then he may have killed her?'

'I'm sorry, but at the moment we don't know what this blood means. We shan't know anything until we can learn her blood group.'

'I don't know it.'

'Would your wife?'

'She's too doped to know anything. For God's sake let her be.'

'Who's your doctor?'

'Fingay.'

Agar tried to find some words of comfort before he left, but he turned away and went out of the room without speaking.

Once outside the house, he pushed his way through the crowd and returned to his car. He drove to the call-box by the cross-roads, went into it and looked in the directory for Dr. Fingay's address.

115

A five-minute drive brought him to a modern, L-shaped house, built in charming pink-grey brick with light red roof tiles.

The doctor was young, in his late twenties, and was dressed in tennis shorts and shirt and obviously on the point of going out. He listened to Agar and then led the way along a passage and through the garage to the surgery beyond.

After a quick search in the top drawer of a metal cabinet the doctor brought out a filing card. 'Yes, I've a note of her blood group, thanks to an accident she had a couple of years ago. She's group O. Does that help you at all?'

'In a way, but only negatively.' Agar sounded as tired as he felt. 'We found blood on some grass on the common. That's been typed AB. As it wasn't hers, presumably it was Krammer's. I suppose the poor kid fought like hell.'

'But if she'd been able to fight that hard, surely someone would have seen her? It's a pretty busy road right through the night.'

'There's a bit of a slope down from the pavement just there. If they'd fallen over and rolled down . . . Except that if they'd fought on the ground the grass and nettles would have shown it and they didn't. Look, could I use your phone to make a call? I'll charge it up to the police.'

'Go right ahead.'

Agar asked for Lettworth Prison and during the wait he accepted both a cigarette and a light from the doctor. When the connexion was made he spoke to the assistant governor he had previously met and he asked for Krammer's blood group, if known. The other said it would obviously take time to find out the information and he'd ring back as soon as possible.

After Agar replaced the receiver the doctor looked at his watch and said he had to go out, but that Agar was to stay as long as he wanted and was there anything more he, Fingay, could do before he went?

Once alone, Agar began to pace the floor of the surgery. After a while he stopped and stared at the glass-fronted cabinet inside of which lay a number of ominous-looking surgical instruments.

The telephone rang. 'We've pulled the doc out of his post-prandial nap and he's checked the records. Krammer's blood group is O,' said the assistant governor.

'What?'

'O for Overlord.'

Agar thanked the other and rang off. He stared at the far wall. If both Sarah Bramswell and Krammer were group O, whose blood was on the grass? Clearly, there were two possible answers. Either it was not Krammer who had attacked and abducted Sarah and there was another sex maniac at large wearing similar patterned shoes or there was another man connected with Krammer's attack. The second alternative being by far the more likely one, he tried to think who it could be. A pedestrian, a motorist? A motorist seemed the obvious answer because if Krammer had stolen a car there would be an explanation of how he had escaped with the girl without being seen. But then where was this second man? He was injured, so why hadn't he reported the assault. Was he dead?

Agar hurriedly left the surgery. He walked through the garage, now with only one car in it, and after thanking the doctor's wife left the house and went back out to his Morris.

* * * * *

'Here is an important announcement,' said the B.B.C. announcer. 'It seems possible that a man or woman, driving a car, may have received injuries last night on the London road in Stoneyacre. Will this person, or anyone who knows about such incident, or will anyone who knows of any man or woman who has been missing since last night, please contact the nearest police station. I will repeat that. It seems possible . . .'

.   .   .   .   .

By 7 p.m. the heat had abated somewhat. In Trafalgar Square three men went swimming in the fountains, on Seascale beach a fashion model wore a topless bathing suit and the cameras clicked like mad, and in Glasgow a Conservative politician was booed. In the search of the countryside surrounding Stoneyacre more than thirty people had collapsed from the heat and physical exhaustion.

At 7.15 p.m. there was a knock on the front door of Adriadnoch House. In the sitting-room Krammer crossed to the bay window, protected with heavy net curtains, from which he could see the front door. Almost immediately he stepped back. 'It's a policeman,' he said calmly. 'A sergeant.'

She gasped.

He spoke slowly. 'They are probably checking every house. Whatever happens, you're not to tell him.'

'I won't,' she muttered.

'There's a chain on the front door. Leave the door on that chain when you speak to him and find out everything he wants. I'll be right behind you, Amelia, and don't forget what a terrible pity it would be if anything had to happen to Sarah now.' There was more knocking on the door. He ignored it and walked to the chair in which she sat. He rested his right hand on her shoulder and began to stroke the side of her neck. 'We're such friends now and it would be awful to spoil that.'

She stood up, her mind chaotic from the emotions of

118

hope and fear. She must make the sergeant realize what was going on. Then something occurred to her. Perhaps he had come because of her telephone call to the vicar's wife? Hope became greater as she convinced herself that that must be it, even though so much time had passed since it had taken place.

She stood up and her legs were trembling. She walked to the door and out into the hall. As she came to a halt before the front door she felt a hand on her right hip. Fingers pressed gently, but insistently, so that she could feel their pressure on her flesh.

'Don't forget,' Krammer whispered.

She tried desperately not to think of those fingers as she opened the door to the extent of the chain. 'What is it?' Her voice was high.

'It's all right, Mrs. Pretty. Sergeant Armstrong, here, from the local police station. Can I have a word with you?'

'What about?'

'Sarah Bramswell, the girl who's missing.'

'What about her?'

'We're going round to every house, Mrs. Pretty, to ask people if they've seen or heard anything suspicious.'

She suffered intense disappointment because this visit had nothing to do with her telephone call to the vicar's wife.

Krammer's fingers moved up her body and seemed to be about to reach for her breast. She shivered, quite uncontrollably. Frantically, she tried to concentrate. She had to save the girl. She had to. . . . Krammer's fingers found her right breast. They did nothing other than rest there, but that was enough.

'Have you seen anything at all suspicious, Mrs. Pretty?'

'No!' she cried out.

'Is anything wrong?'

'No.'

'Suppose you let me come in and have a word with you.'

Wildly, struggling to concentrate, she could only think of one thing to do. To be so rude to the sergeant that he must guess the truth. 'Go away,' she shouted. Krammer's fingers seemed to have become red hot: they scorched her flesh. She struggled to drag his hand away from herself, but lacked all strength. 'I didn't ask you to come here,' she continued. 'Stop worrying me.'

'The young girl, Mrs. Pretty . . .'

'Don't bother me about some little slut from the village. Get off my land. Get off, d'you hear.'

There was a silence. During it, all three of them were still. The sergeant stood outside the door, under the ugly Gothic porch, Amelia stood inside, shaking, her chunky face flushed red and her right hand ineffectually pulling at Krammer's right hand, and Krammer stood behind her, leaning gently against her.

When the sergeant spoke again he allowed his voice to express his hostility. 'You haven't seen or heard anything?'

'That's what I said. Now get off my land.'

'All right. It's very fortunate for you, Mrs. Pretty, that it's not your daughter, isn't it?' He walked away. The old bitch was pottier than ever, he said to himself.

They heard the slam of a car door. The engine was started and revved hard immediately, the note dying away slightly as the car moved off.

Krammer's fingers dropped away from her breast. Slowly, the tears formed in her eyes and very soon they spilled down her cheeks. She brushed them off with a hand that shook.

'I'm so sorry,' said Krammer.

She turned away so that he should not see her face and

the expression on it, but she was painfully certain that he did not need to.

'Shall we have dinner?' he asked.

'All right,' she answered dully.

She led the way through to the kitchen. Once inside, she pointed to the large tin of tongue on the table and asked him to open it. He did so, with the same concentrated care with which he did everything.

She went into the larder and brought out the lemon meringue pie she had made before tea.

'Sarah's going to adore that,' he said, as she put the pie on the table. 'She says she prefers it to anything but praline ice cream. I said I'd try to get some of that for her. D'you think we can? Will they have it in any of the shops?'

'I don't know. I never eat ice cream.'

'She's a wonderful girl, Amelia, when you get to know her. She was so frightened at first, but so brave. Then, when she got over her fright, she became gay and she laughs when I play the fool with her. My wife and I never had children. I didn't think I wanted any, but I would give anything to have had one like Sarah. She's so bright and intelligent.'

'She . . . Isn't she afraid of you?'

'Of course she isn't, not now.' He unlocked a drawer, took out a carving knife and fork and began to carve the tongue. 'I suppose it's difficult for you to believe that, because of what happened to those other girls. But, you see, she doesn't really know what did happen to them. She's too innocent. Amelia, can you understand what it means to meet such innocence?'

She shook her head.

'It's as if . . . I can't really describe it.' Krammer carefully arranged the cut tongue on a plate. 'She said she was hungry, so I'll give her three slices and a nice helping of potato salad. I told her she ought to have some green vegetables, but she said she never had any when she was having a party meal. Can you get her tray ready, Amelia? I thought she might like some pickles, but she told me she didn't because they were like curry. I don't think they really are, do you?'

Moving as though in a dream-shackled world, she made up the tray for Sarah and put it close to him. He placed the plate of tongue on it. She watched him turn to his right and cut a large slice of lemon pie.

He checked the contents of the tray. 'There, that seems to be everything. I'll take it up to her.'

'I'm coming with you. I want to see her and speak to her.'

He frowned slightly. 'I . . . I don't know.'

'I'm coming up.'

'All right. But if she's asleep we won't disturb her. She's been sleeping a great deal as if she was really tired right out. I like to see her asleep, she's so beautiful. That reminds me. She asked for something to read: have you any books she would like?'

'There aren't any books in the house but the ones I read as a child.'

'Let me have one or two of those.'

'But children read such different things these days.'

'That doesn't matter. I'm sure she's the kind of girl who'll like the old favourites. When I was young I longed for some books, but we were too poor to have any. Now, let's go up.' He picked up the tray.

She followed him out of the kitchen and felt breathless because of the sense of tension within herself.

He went up the stairs, all his movements more precise than usual because of the need to keep the tray steady. They reached the top of the stairs, turned right, and went along the corridor. He stopped in front of the girl's bedroom and waited until Mrs. Pretty was with him, then he handed her the tray.

Her hands were shaking so much that when she took the tray the water slopped over the glass.

He knocked gently on the door and listened. There was no sound. He knocked again, a little more loudly. Still, there was no answer. 'Sarah,' he called out, 'are you ready for your dinner? There's a lovely big piece of lemon pie for you.'

The silence continued.

He looked at Mrs. Pretty and smiled. 'She must be sleeping heavily. I'll just have a quick look.' He took a key from his coat pocket, put it in the lock, and turned it. He opened the door until he could look inside.

She moved to her left so that she also could see the girl, but as she moved so he stepped back and shut the door. He locked it.

'Please let me——' she began.

He interrupted her. 'Isn't it wonderful how the body can comfort itself with sleep?'

'Please, I want to see she's all right.'

'I'll take the tray, Amelia, and leave it in my room for the moment and then I can give it to her when she wakes up.' He took the tray from her. 'Could you put a fresh towel out for her? She said she might like a bath and so she can have one tonight.'

She gave him the tray. He carried it into the bedroom next to the one Sarah was in. Whilst he was out of sight she put her ear against the door of the bedroom in front of her, but she could hear nothing. When he returned he came towards her as if to touch her and she stepped back from the door and flinched. He looked sadly at her.

Once downstairs, she laid the table in the dining-room for their meal. Everything else had failed, so now she had to get him so drunk that he became incapable. She brought a bottle of whisky and a bottle of Beaune from the pantry, put the wine in the dining-room, and took the whisky into the sitting-room.

She persuaded him to have two whiskies before the meal and made certain they were strong ones. They finished the bottle of wine with the meal and he had five glassfuls to her one. After the meal she went into the sitting-room and brought back the whisky. She poured him out a very strong drink.

'I love to eat and drink as we have,' he said, sprawling in the ladder-back chair. 'I couldn't afford a bottle of wine until I was thirty. I knew one couldn't be a gentleman until one had learned to drink wine. I didn't pay much for my first bottle and it tasted like vinegar.'

She noticed he was slurring his words.

He went on talking. 'It's lovely, though, when you can afford nice wine.' He looked across at her. 'You aren't drinking, Amelia. You must, because it isn't right to drink on my own.' He stood up and poured her out a whisky.

'That's much too strong,' she protested.

'Nonsense, it's not nearly as strong as the one you gave me.' He laughed. 'Perhaps you're trying to get me drunk?'

She felt that the shock his words caused must show on her face. 'No. No, of course I'm not,' she said hurriedly.

He handed her the glass. 'Don't take too long about this one because then we can have the fun of another. Shall I tell you something, Amelia? This is the first time for years I've really felt comfortable. You've made me all relaxed.'

She drank the whisky, disliking it because it was so strong. But she knew that if she finished it he would have another and then perhaps yet one more and by then he must be affected. What was she going to do? Take the key from him and get the girl out of the room and away from the house? Or call the police in? Must she try to bind him, or would the alcohol make certain he did not move?

When she had emptied her glass he poured out two more drinks. They were even stronger than the previous two. He raised his glass. 'You're so lovely, Amelia, I drink to you.'

She stared at him.

'Please don't stop me saying that. You're the kind of person who lives to be worshipped. If I could have met you years ago everything would have been so different: so very different.'

She drank and soon became aware of the fact that her own faculties were being affected by the alcohol. She tried to force her mind to remain logical and constant, but it kept slipping away. Once, she even found herself wildly thinking that this was her late husband who sat opposite her in those clothes she knew so well.

She was uncertain how much time passed or, even, whether she had had more drinks, but then her mind cleared enough to tell her she must go to bed. As she stood up, he did the same with an instant awareness of what good manners dictated.

'I must come upstairs and lock your door,' he said, his words still more slurred. 'You do understand why I have to do that, don't you?'

She did not answer.

They climbed the stairs. Half-way up, on the small half-landing, she caught the heel of her left shoe in the worn patch of the carpet and fell on to the banisters. Immediately he caught hold of her and then used his unusual strength to help her upright. He left his hands on her. She began to tremble and the trembling grew until it was as if she had a fever. In a wild desperation she tried to struggle free, but could not. She moaned, a deep, wavering sound which she could do nothing to prevent.

He suddenly let go of her and she almost fell again, but was able to grab the banisters in time. She went up the second flight of stairs as quickly as she dared, desperately conscious of the fact that he was immediately behind her. She turned right and went past Sarah's room to the bathroom. When she returned he was standing in the centre of the corridor, arms crossed.

She almost ran to get past him.

'Good night, Amelia,' he said.

She went into her room and shut the door. She heard the key being inserted and turned and the lock click shut. Her body began to tremble once more. She crossed to the mirror on top of the dressing-table and stared at her face.

It was a square, ugly, time-battered face, showing the harsh marks of sorrow and loneliness, but also there, for those who could read, were the marks of passion. It was the ugly face of a woman who could find the flames of immortality in the act of love. Helen's character must have been like hers. Perhaps Helen's face was, as well. Tradition said that Helen was ravishingly attractive, but pure physical beauty so seldom concealed her kind of physical fire. Paris might have seen in Menelaus' wife's ugly face the same kind of beautiful passion as her late husband had in hers.

She undressed and stood naked in front of the dressing-table and the mirror. Her body sagged and her breasts were pendulous, but such imperfections had not stopped the fires burning.

She began to cry.

.   .   .   .   .

The police had been lucky when they found the roll of binder twine, but it was some time before they knew this.

Two civilian scientists spent all Sunday afternoon and evening in a swelteringly hot London analysing the twine, trying to break it down into its constituent parts so that firms all over the country could be questioned to see if this was their product. The task was obviously going to take days and therefore was a bitterly discouraging one because there was no time available. It was now almost twenty-four hours since the girl had disappeared. In seventy-two hours she would probably have died a most terrible, degrading death.

At 10.12 p.m., a little before the two men were due to be relieved by others who would carry on working through-out the night, the younger of them suggested they should break off their present task and unravel the entire ball and measure it. This could have been done before, but they had been too eager to start work immediately on the twine in case, by a miracle, they had been able to find out anything important right away.

The ball of twine seemed endless and it became obvious they should never have attempted such a task in the labor-atory, even though it was forty feet long. Their reliefs arrived and made a number of caustic comments. Then, when nearly at the end of the roll, they found a plastic tag, bearing a trademark, through which the twine passed.

'Pray God it helps,' said someone quietly.

·   ·   ·   ·   ·

Agar arrived home at 1 a.m. on Monday morning. As soon as he was inside the door he took off his shoes, but he was only half-way up the stairs when his wife called out from their bedroom. 'Bill, food's in the oven.'

He hurried up and into the bedroom. 'I don't know I really want to eat anything,' he said, as he dropped his shoes on to the floor.

'You must eat. I'll bet you've only had sandwiches since I last saw you.' She brushed a loose strand of hair from her eyes. 'What about the case?'

He shrugged his shoulders. 'We've found one or two things but we've no idea yet what they mean.'

'Why did they put out that latest broadcast appeal and ask for news of anyone who's missing?'

He told her.

'If you could find the driver he might really be able to help you?'

'If there is one, Carry.'

'But you've just said you don't believe the alternative—that there's another sex maniac loose.'

He took a packet of cigarettes out of his pocket and lit one. 'If there was a car and the driver's missing why in hell don't we know? Why hasn't a wife told us her husband's vanished? Why doesn't a landlady say her lodger's disappeared?'

'This driver must live on his own.'

'Maybe. But where is he now? Krammer can't be hiding him as well as the girl.'

She changed the conversation, belatedly trying to ease his mental tension. 'Go and eat, Bill, and hurry back up to bed. I suppose you'll have to be off pretty early in the morning?'

'Just as soon as I can drag myself out of bed, but six at the very latest.' He yawned heavily. 'I won't have anything to eat. . . .'

'You're not coming to bed until you've had something. There's cottage pie in the oven and some mousetrap cheese in the larder.'

He yawned again and then, shoeless, went down to the kitchen. He served himself some cottage pie and began to eat. He knew it was ridiculous to do so, but he felt guilty about going to bed. For a few hours he would be peacefully sleeping during all of which time the girl would be tortured. The contrast between his state and the girl's made him want to suffer the pains of staying awake, when all of his body was aching for sleep, because by doing so he would be suffering a little while she was suffering a lot.

.   .   .   .   .   .

By 7 a.m. it was obvious that the day was going to be one of those dull, overcast ones which so often destroyed the Britisher's belief in the existence of summer.

Mrs. Pretty, in a cotton print dress that did not try to fit her, waited in the sitting-room. Soon, if only there was a letter to deliver, the postman would arrive. All the plans she had made the previous morning could come to fruition.

She looked at her watch and the time was 7.16. There must be some post for her today. She found she was clenching her fists. Was she quite certain what she was going to say? What would she do if the man didn't have enough common sense to act exactly as she suggested?

The red van came up the drive, round the central flower bed, and stopped. As she watched, the driver climbed out with a couple of envelopes in his hand. She felt so sweeping an excitement that there was a sick feeling in the middle of her body.

She went into the hall, trying to move without sound. She looked round herself. The hall, the stairs, the half-landing, and the landing, were empty. Krammer was nowhere in sight.

If only the front door didn't squeak too much everything would be all right. She mustn't open the door too quickly, then, but on the other hand she mustn't delay the opening so long that the postman began his walk back to the van.

She gently slid back the two bolts and the chain, unlocked the door, turned the handle and pulled. She came face to face with the postman who was holding out the letters ready to put them into a letter-box that had suddenly retreated.

He was young, with a jolly, round face and curly hair that sprouted in all directions from under his cap. He stared at her with open bewilderment.

She was about to speak, to let loose all the words that crowded her mind, when she heard a cough which came from behind her: it was an apologetic, muted cough, little more than the clearing of a throat, the kind of cough a man made when he wanted to draw attention to himself without intruding.

Her face expressed her bitter, agonizing feeling of impotency. The postman stared at her. 'Something wrong?' he asked anxiously.

'No,' she replied, 'nothing.'

'You're quite certain?'

'Yes.'

'Well, I just thought . . . Two letters for you today.'

She held out her hand and he gave them to her. She automatically noticed that the top one was an airmail letter from the U.S.A., which meant her late husband's cousin was writing and moaning about something.

'Not such a nice day,' said the postman.

'No.'

'Terrible thing about that girl, isn't it?'

'Yes.'

'Well, if I don't get on with it the head postmaster will tell me all about it when I gets back. 'Morning.'

She watched him walk back to his van, climb in, and slam the door shut. She stood quite still as he drove on round the circular flower bed and then out of sight down the drive. Slowly, she shut the door.

'Thank you so much for being nice and not saying anything,' murmured Krammer.

. . . . .

Throughout the country the police interviewed people to try to discover who had produced the ball of twine. At 10.54 a.m. a uniformed sergeant spoke to the manager of a small firm in the Lippenshaw area of Birmingham.

The sergeant handed Webster, the manager, two photographs. 'This is the plastic tab, sir, enlarged, of course. The twine was threaded through it.'

Webster studied the photograph. 'That came from us,' he said immediately. 'The device is a crossed pair of anchors with a capstan on top—not that you can begin to tell what it's meant to be. The firm was once in Bristol in the shipchandler business.'

'Right, sir, then I've a few questions for you.'

'What's the trouble?'

'The Krammer case.'

'Good God!' The manager was shocked to be brought even this close to so terrible a crime.

'The ball of twine was found at the spot where we're certain Krammer picked the girl up. We want to know how the twine got there?'

'What was the name of the place?'

'Stoneyacre.'

'I just don't know. We produce a hell of a lot of this binder twine and how one ball turned up there when it did . . . I just don't know.'

'This ball was brand new and didn't look as if it had ever been handled. We wondered if you have men who travel with it?'

'Two in the north and two in the south. They handle our other lines as well, of course.'

'Is one of your travellers in the south missing or in hospital from an accident?'

Webster looked bewildered, but quickly picked up one of the two telephone receivers and spoke to someone. There was a short wait, during which Webster drummed on his desk with the fingers of his right hand, then a tall, thin, almost bald man came into the room.

'Who's travelling in the south, Tom?' asked Webster.

'Avanti and Chalmers. Avanti's doing Cornwall through to Dorset, Wiltshire and Gloucestershire, and Chalmers is doing Hampshire, Berkshire, and Oxford through to Kent and Essex.'

'Where would Chalmers be now?' asked the sergeant.

The man studied a sheet of paper in his hand. 'Today and tomorrow he'll be based at Raleton.'

'Do you know whether he is there or not?'

The manager explained the reason for the question. 'It's the Krammer case, Tom. The police think maybe one of our travellers is missing or met with an accident.'

'I haven't heard of anything.'

'But would you necessarily have heard?' asked the sergeant. 'Today's Monday, so he wasn't working yesterday. Is he married?'

'No. Not that he shouldn't be, from all accounts.'

'Any idea where he stays in Raleton?'

'At the commercial hotel, near the railway station, but damned if I can tell you the name of it.'

The sergeant asked if he might use the telephone. He dialled his police station, spoke to the duty inspector, and reported what he had learned. After the call was over, and he had replaced the receiver, he questioned the manager again. 'Does Chalmers use a car?'

'The firm runs one for him.'

'What make and registration number?'

It was the tall, thin man who answered. 'Tony had a Ford Capri—the model they don't make any more. I'll have to go back to the records for the registration number.'

There was a short pause. 'D'you really think he's somehow mixed up in the Krammer case?' asked Webster.

Twelve

As the information came through to them the police were able to reconstruct what had happened to Chalmers. He had been driving from London to Raleton late Saturday night and for some reason he had stopped in the middle of Stoneyacre Common. There he was attacked by Krammer and at some time one of the balls of binder twine he was carrying in the car had spilled out and rolled across the narrow pavement and down the slight slope into the clump of stinging nettles. The Railway Arms Hotel had been expecting him late Saturday night: because he was an old and trusted customer, and because there was no night porter, they left a key to the back door under a flower-pot in the courtyard. When the staff discovered on Sunday morning that he had not arrived the previous night they had not been worried since, being a commercial traveller, he had on other occasions been unavoidably delayed. The staff had heard the police appeal to report missing persons, but at no time, not even by Monday morning, did they consider Chalmers to be a missing person.

There was a conference of senior police officials in Stoneyacre Village Hut just before midday. Facts were correlated and cross-referenced diagrams were used to record those facts known and all relevant times, then the meeting was thrown open for general discussion.

Agar stood up. The assistant chief constable looked at him with an expression that suggested dislike and he muttered something to the commander from Scotland Yard who sat with him and Detective Superintendent Pearce on the dais.

'For some reason, sir,' said Agar to Pearce, who was nominally in charge of the meeting, 'Chalmers stopped the car on the common. It could have been because Krammer was acting as if he needed help, but after all the warnings that were put out that doesn't seem very likely. It could have been because he saw Krammer struggling with the girl, but surely in that case he would have armed himself with something and given a good account of himself. The third possibility is that the stop was involuntary with perhaps something going wrong with the car.'

'Yes,' said Pearce, in a neutral tone of voice.

'Let's say the car was in trouble, but not too seriously: it was still a runner. There's a lot of trouble on the journey and in the end he stops in the middle of Stoneyacre Common to see if there's anything he can do. Krammer, who has been hiding nearby, sees this as the chance he's been desperately needing. He comes up behind Chalmers and lays him out with something heavy. Chalmers rolls down the slope and his head ends up where we found the blood. Just after that, or just after Krammer has dragged the unconscious Chalmers into the car, Sarah Bramswell comes along the pavement. Krammer persuades her to get into the car. He drives off.

'In that case, sir, it must be worth our questioning all garages in the area about a Ford Capri. The car was never produced in great numbers and it's got the kind of lines that will stick in people's minds. If Krammer did have to call at a garage we might get a lead on the direction in which he went.'

The detective superintendent looked at the commander,

135

who nodded. 'All right,' he said. 'You organize that. Give it a hundred-mile circle to start with.'

'Right, sir.'

'And get the thing rolling now.'

Agar left the meeting, glad to get away from so many tired, frustrated, despondent men. He drove the short distance to the operations van and began telephoning sectional D.I.s of J.A.P.

·   ·   ·   ·   ·

The manager of the London Road Garage, just past Borley Woods and twenty-five miles from Raleton and the coast, said that although none of the day staff could remember a Ford Capri, the garage had been open all night Saturday and the night man, Yewton, might be able to tell the police something. Yewton lived half a mile away.

The two constables drove half a mile back in the direction of Stoneyacre and found the cottage without difficulty. Mrs. Yewton at first indignantly objected to waking her husband, who had been on duty all night, but when they explained their enquiries had to do with the Krammer case she had no further objections and went off to shake some life into him.

Several minutes later Yewton came into the room wearing a pair of oil-stained trousers over some almost equally dirty pyjamas. He had the dazed appearance of a man who had been suddenly awakened from a very deep sleep.

'Sorry to bust in on you like this,' said the elder of the two constables.

'Me too.'

'We're looking for a Ford Capri that may have been on the road Saturday night or early Sunday morning.'

Yewton shuffled round the room, in bedroom slippers too big for him, looking for a cigarette. In the end he asked his wife for one. The younger constable offered a packet and they all smoked.

'Give us a cup of tea, love,' Yewton said to his wife.

She asked the policemen if they would like some tea and they said they would. After she had gone out of the room Yewton spoke to the others. 'What's the Capri look like? There's so many Fords these days a bloke can't tell one from t'other.'

He was handed a photograph.

'One like that, eh? Don't see many of them and that's a fact. But I'll tell you this, there was one come last Saturday night to the garage.'

'When?'

'Well, I wouldn't put a minute to it and that's the truth, but if I said it was around midnight I wouldn't be telling no lie.'

'What happened?'

'The engine was in trouble: popping like it'd eaten a load of onions. I said I wasn't no mechanic, but the bloke wanted me to do something and I found a plug lead missing. And d'you know what? I'll never forget it, not to me dying day. Never so much as a tanner for what I did: not a bloody tanner.'

'Which way did he drive off?'

'Went on towards Raleton.'

'Any idea how many were in the car?'

'There was the driver, like I said.'

'No one else?'

'I didn't see no one. There weren't no one in the passenger seat and the back seat ain't big enough for much, is it?'

'Did you see the driver's face?'

'I saw a bit of it. He was wearing some uniform hat, so I couldn't see much, but . . .' Yewton became silent as he thought back.

The constable produced a photograph of Krammer, full face, covered the top half of the head with his left hand and then showed it to Yewton.

Yewton spoke with more interest. 'That's 'im, right enough. No passion in them kind of lips, I always say. Something to do with the sex bloke?'

The constable removed his hand from the photograph.

Yewton stared at it. 'But that's the bloke?'

'Yes.'

'Then it was 'im what called at the station? With the girl in the back of the car, likely? And I didn't bleeding well recognize 'im!' He groaned.

.   .   .   .   .   .

Agar, Detective Inspector Raydon, Detective Superintendent Pearce, the commander, the assistant chief constable, and a uniformed chief superintendent all stared at the road map.

The assistant chief constable spoke. 'If Krammer drove from that petrol station towards Raleton he probably reached the town and we ought to shift the concentrated search down there.'

The commander nodded. 'That's what I'd do.'

'Pearce?'

'Yes, sir.'

The A.C.C. stared out through the window of the operations van. After a while he spoke again. 'All right, then. Thin out all searchers up here and get them down there as quickly as you can. What sort of transport can we muster?'

'Army trucks and some London Transport buses, sir,'

replied the chief superintendent. 'Two hours should see most of 'em shifted.'

The commander stubbed his finger down on the coast line on the map. 'I'll take any money you like he's not in a town. We'd have picked him up by now. He's hiding out somewhere in the countryside: an abandoned quarry, a wood. Goddamn it, there's a car, Krammer, the poor kid, and Chalmers, all missing. Is he in some isolated home? But the reports are that every single house for miles has been checked. Where the hell is he? How long has he had the girl now?'

'Coming up to thirty-six hours, sir,' said Agar harshly.

'Thirty-six hours. God knows how long they've seemed to Sarah Bramswell.'

.   .   .   .   .

Mrs. Pretty picked up the telephone and dialled 436. The ringing tones began. She heard a sound and looked up to see Krammer on the half-landing.

The ringing tones stopped as the call was answered. 'Good morning, can I help you?'

'It's Mrs. Pretty here.'

'Good morning, Mrs. Pretty, not such a nice day. What will it be for tomorrow? We've some very nice pork chops or some lovely English lamb chops. Mr. Butler was only just saying how you'd probably like the pork chops, Mrs. Pretty.'

'I want a leg of lamb and three pounds of pork sausages.'

'Did you say a *leg* of lamb?'

'Yes.'

'And three pounds of pork sausages?'

'Yes.'

'No chops?'

'No.'

'Very well, Mrs. Pretty. We'll deliver a *leg* of English lamb and three pounds of pork sausages tomorrow morning.'

Mrs. Pretty replaced the receiver. In the fifteen years she had lived in Stoneyacre she had never bought a joint because she hated cold meat, nor had she ever bought sausages because she loathed them, hot or cold. Both the butcher and the over-refined woman at the cash desk knew that her meat order had never been anything but steak, chops, or cutlets. But Krammer, waiting patiently on the half-landing, didn't know that.

She picked up the receiver again and dialled 222, the number of the general store. 'It's Mrs. Pretty,' she said, as soon as the connexion was made. 'I want three tins of salmon, two pounds of back rashers, a pound of marmalade, a dozen boxes of matches, and two pounds of onions, please.'

'What was that last thing, Mrs. Pretty?'

'Onions.'

'But . . . but you never have onions.'

'That's right.'

There was a pause. 'Two pounds of onions, then.'

She replaced the receiver. The store knew very well that she hated onions and refused to eat anything with onions in it. They must think it exceptionally odd that she should suddenly ask for two pounds of them. The owner of the general store was a cousin of Butler and they frequently saw each other.

Krammer came down the stairs. She watched the lithe way in which he walked and thought that that was how a cat walked. He had changed out of the suit and was now wearing grey flannel trousers and a blazer with the crest of her late husband's college over the breast pocket.

'I hope you don't mind?' said Krammer.

'Mind?'

'You seemed to be looking at this blazer as if I shouldn't be wearing it?'

'It's quite all right.'

He stood close to her, reached over, and took hold of her right hand and held it in both of his. 'I wouldn't do anything you didn't want me to, I promise you that.'

She tried to release her hand, but his grip tightened.

'She's enjoying the books of yours,' he said. 'At first she thought they looked much too old-fashioned, but when she did start to read one she couldn't put it down. She's such a wonderful girl, always so alive. Just like you, Amelia.'

'I'm too old to be alive.'

He shook his head and smiled. 'Will you tell me something?' he asked.

'If I can.'

'Do you like me?'

'Yes, of course.'

'You're so kind to me. D'you know, this is the first house I've ever been in where I've really been liked by two people. Sarah said this morning that she liked me very much and it made me feel . . . feel worth while for once.'

'But your wife loves you.'

'I must tell you about her. I've been wanting to, right from the beginning, but I haven't had the courage.'

'I don't . . .'

'I married her because she was so desperately lonely and I was the same: we thought that by getting married we could both lose our loneliness. But it just didn't work out and I couldn't love her. You hated me at the beginning, but now I can tell you don't hate me. I am right, aren't I? You don't hate me?'

'Of course I don't. Look, please let me see Sarah.'

He ignored her request. 'I knew I was right. Sometimes

when I touch you you tremble. People who hate each other don't do that.'

He seemed to be about to come closer to her. She stepped back and pulled at her hand which he slowly let go.

'Don't ever be nasty to me?' he said.

She did not try to answer. At all costs she must keep him in a good temper—but how was she to do that and not be a traitor to herself?

.   .   .   .   .   .

They found Chalmers at 2.33 that afternoon. He lay in the same position in which he had been dumped by Krammer. The dried blood caked the side of his face and he was not perceptibly breathing. The army corporal who found him reported him as dead and the other searchers who crowded round were not going to argue on that score. A police sergeant crashed his way through the wood and ordered the searchers to stand back and to keep clear the area between the body and the road.

The police doctor arrived, made a quick examination, and to the surprise of everyone said that the man was still alive. An ambulance took Chalmers to Palmersh.

Agar arrived at the hospital at 3.10 and waited impatiently in the almoner's office for nearly an hour. At the end of that time he was allowed to go up to the room in which Chalmers lay supinely, his skull bandaged. Agar spoke to the doctor. 'Well?'

'He may not recover consciousness for days, if ever.'

Agar swore.

'He won't be any help to you. His skull's received severe fractures and there's extensive bruising. He's lost a lot of blood which we've replaced, but he's been lying out for almost thirty-six hours, so we're struggling against exposure as well as everything else. If the weather had been at all inclement he would have died some time back.'

'Is there any chance at all he might suddenly come to?'

'It's always possible, but for the records I don't suppose he will.'

'I'll have a man standing by in case.'

'D'you think Chalmers could tell you where Krammer's taken the girl?'

'The odds against it are incalculable,' said Agar bitterly, 'but right now we're clutching hard at anything.'

'I wonder why the human race hasn't yet learned what to do with its sexual rogues,' said the doctor sadly. 'Still, one of these days I suppose it will be possible and legal to operate and remove a portion of their brain and they'll trot round the place as harmless as a two-year-old.'

And what use will that be to Sarah Bramswell? thought Agar, with bitter anger.

. . . . . .

The clouds disappeared as night came on, in the infuriating way they so often did in the summer.

In the kitchen Mrs. Pretty beat up the eggs in the saucepan with a fork, as her mother had always taught her to do: real scrambled eggs could only be made with a fork.

Krammer was standing by the doorway into the hall. 'She's not been able to have scrambled eggs very often at home,' he said. 'Her parents aren't very well off and it takes up so many eggs.'

'Does she like a touch of pepper?'

'I never asked her. I'll nip upstairs and ask her.'

'Let me come with you?'

'No.'

'Why not? Why won't you let me see her? What's wrong?'

'Nothing's wrong, Amelia, nothing.'

'Please, please, I want to see her.'

'Not now. I'll tell you why at supper, but not now.' He left the kitchen before she could say anything more.

She went on gently stirring the eggs as they slowly scrambled. How could the butcher and the general store have failed to realize the true meaning of her telephone calls of the morning? It made her sick to think how stupid people were being. And yet, at the same time as she cursed their stupidity, she was becoming more and more uncertain whether she should summon help in the way she had been trying to: if Krammer had the slightest inkling that the police were coming he would kill the girl. At least, that was what he had threatened to do. But surely a man as sensitive as he was couldn't really do such a beastly, filthy thing? Then she remembered his trial and the way in which those girls had died after four days. Desperately, she told herself that something had changed in him. People, even the worst people, could change. That was what a lot of life was about: a chance to let people change from bad to good.

He returned to the kitchen. 'Sarah says no pepper, thanks, because it burns her mouth.' He sat down on the edge of the kitchen table. 'This may sound stupid, Amelia, but just finding out whether she wants salt and pepper makes me feel like a father.' He smiled.

She silently prayed he would continue to feel like a father. She added a pinch of salt to the eggs, stirred them for a little longer, and then spooned them out on to the toast which was already buttered.

He stood up and picked up the plate and put it on the tray. With a care that was almost ludicrous he checked that there was water, knife and fork, and three chocolate biscuits there. Satisfied, he smiled at her again before leaving to take the tray upstairs.

144

Mrs. Pretty prepared their own meal. She opened two tins of Chili Con Carne and added certain spices. This had been a meal of which her late husband had been very fond.

They ate in the dining-room and shared another bottle of wine, only on this occasion he poured the wine out and made certain they halved it.

Their conversation was desultory until they had both finished eating. Then he coughed twice, looked at her, fiddled with a fork, and finally began to speak. 'I used to have to do it, Amelia. I tried to stop myself, but I couldn't. I hated myself, but I couldn't stop. I don't suppose you can imagine what it's like to hate yourself as I hated myself.

'Because I couldn't stop myself, I tried to become even filthier to prove to myself I didn't care. I thought of acts so ghastly no human being could do them . . . And I did them. I hated myself so much I couldn't bear to look in a mirror. In the end I wanted to kill myself in the most humiliating way I could think of.

'I had been terrified of being caught. But secretly I must have wanted it because when they got me, everything suddenly became different. I had longed to punish myself but hadn't dared, now someone was doing it for me. I fought as hard as I could and denied everything because the more I fought against the punishment, the more wonderful I knew it would be when I received it. When the judge condemned me to death I felt as if I'd been washed clean.

'They didn't kill me, but sent me to prison. That didn't matter: I was still being punished. But the people in prison wouldn't let me stay feeling clean. They'd done terrible things themselves, but they treated me as untouchable. It was ghastly what they did to me. I couldn't stand it. I had to get away because they made the punishment too great, even for me.

'When I escaped I didn't know where I was going. Time didn't exist: the world didn't exist. I came to suddenly on a common near a man who was looking at the engine of his car. I found a bar of iron and hit him with it because I needed his car. I put him in the boot and I was about to drive away when I saw Sarah walking towards me. She looked so lovely, so peaceful, so virginal, that I suddenly knew I had to do something to prove to myself that I had already received enough punishment to clean me through and through, even though I had escaped from prison before my punishment was over. It was like seeing writing in the sky. I had to take Sarah and live with her for four days without touching her so that I would know I was cured. D'you understand?'

'I . . . I think so.'

'I had to give myself the chance of being a beast to prove to myself I no longer was.'

'But her parents?'

'I know. But when Sarah goes back to them think how wonderful their joy will be. They'll forget all their sorrow. And I shall have found myself. It's been a miracle of rebirth for me: every time I've done some little task for Sarah I've discovered the divine joys of serving. In prison, on Sundays, we used to go to church. Most of the men went because it was better than sitting in the cells: but I went to learn about the beauty of serving. Amelia, will they forgive me for bringing Sarah here when they know why I did it?'

'I . . . I don't know.'

'But you understand now?'

'I think so.'

'You've learned, since you tried to call for help?'

'Yes.' She looked straight at him. 'Suppose I had succeeded. Would you have killed her?'

'I'd have to have done. If I couldn't prove myself to

myself it would all have been worse than before.' He reached across the table and laid his hand on hers. 'Let's not talk like that. When a man finds himself, Amelia, it's a miracle.'

Two hours later, after watching television almost as though they were a normal couple enjoying a normal evening, they went to bed.

After going to the bathroom she was locked into her bedroom by Krammer. She undressed slowly and when she was naked she stared down at her body and was about to touch it when she jerked her hand away. She put on her cotton nightdress and had pulled back the corner of the bedclothes when there was a knock on the door. 'Amelia,' Krammer called out.

'What?' she demanded, her voice shrill.

He unlocked the door and entered.

'Get out,' she shouted. 'Get out.'

He looked at her, his lips slightly apart and his pale blue eyes unmoving. After several seconds he walked slowly towards her. She retreated until the back of her knees were caught by the edge of the mattress and she fell on to the bed. She lay there, breathing in deep, shuddering gasps.

He bent down and kissed her. With a last, desperate attempt she fought to free herself, but his strength was too great for her and she could not break free. Abruptly, she could fight no longer because life was bursting through fifteen years of barrenness. She returned his kiss with violent passion and grabbed his right hand and pulled it down until she could push her right breast against it.

He suddenly stood up. 'You're too nice,' he said. He turned and went out of the room and to her the sound of the lock clicking shut was a peal of shattering thunder.

.   .   .   .   .

Butler, the butcher, and his wife were two of the most respectable people in Stoneyacre. They were so respectable that although they had been married twenty-eight years neither of them had ever lewdly gazed upon the nakedness of the other. People who knew them said that their eighteen-year-old son posed an insoluble mystery.

Butler gazed at his wife, in her bed a chaste four feet away. 'Mrs. Pretty is worse than ever.'

'Is she?' asked Mrs. Butler, who revelled in the miseries of others. 'But then she's not a righteous person.'

'She ordered a leg of lamb and three pounds of pork sausages. And you know what she's always said before.'

'Well, I never.'

'More than that, Tom says she ordered onions from him, although she's always refused anything with onions in it.'

'If she's gone really mad, maybe her house will come up for sale. I wonder what it would fetch?'

He allowed his suspicious nature to show. 'More than we'll ever be able to afford.'

'Maybe,' she answered, in the tones of a woman who knew precisely where she was going.

. . . . .

At midnight police H.Q. still had lights on in at least half the rooms. Tired men tried to force their sleep-starved brains to go on working.

In his room Agar finished writing a report and put his pen down. He rested his elbows on the desk and his chin on the palms of his hands. He closed his eyes and was immediately asleep. When, only seconds later, Clanton came into the room, he awoke with a start and the guilty certainty that he had been asleep for hours.

'Anything moving?' asked Clanton.

'I've been on to all sections of J.A.P. and there isn't a Ford Capri among the lot of 'em.'

Clanton sat down behind his desk and yawned. 'God, what does a bed look like?'

'Where in the name of hell can that car be?'

Clanton looked at the wall calendar. 'Forty-nine hours now, Bill. He must have started on the kid by now.'

'I spend my time trying not to think about it.'

'Forty-nine hours and we aren't any nearer finding the girl than when we started.'

'Further away. We concentrated on searching the Stoney-acre area: now we know he reached that garage and drove off towards Raleton, so we've had to alter the centre of our search.'

Clanton fiddled with a pencil. 'If we found her in the morning, Bill, after fifty-eight hours, what state d'you reckon she'd be in?'

'God knows! And what about her mind? Would that be shocked beyond repair?' Agar slammed his clenched fist down on the table. 'Where the bloody hell's the car?'

Thirteen

When Mrs. Pretty first met Krammer on Tuesday morning her face flushed so heavily that she turned away, but he appeared not to have noticed anything.

She hurried along to the bathroom and then, ten minutes later, went down to the kitchen. Krammer followed her and watched her prepare to cook breakfast.

'Sarah doesn't want a fried egg,' he said. 'She asked if she could have two boiled eggs and then some strawberry jam on the bread and butter.'

'What about cornflakes?'

'I'll just go upstairs and ask her.' He left the kitchen.

She half filled a saucepan with warm water and put it on the cooker. Today was the third day, tomorrow was the fourth. What was going to happen after that? Would they drag Krammer back to jail, to be persecuted to death by the other prisoners who were careless that he was a changed man? Would people ever have the wit to see that he had changed so much he was no longer the criminal they had sent to prison for the rest of his life? They couldn't, they musn't, lock him away for ever. When a man lost his reason and had to be sent to a mental hospital he received treatment and if he recovered he was allowed to return as a free man to the world: they must be made to understand that Krammer was totally recovered.

He came running into the kitchen. 'Who's that?' he shouted. He grabbed hold of her arm and his fingers gripped her flesh so harshly she groaned.

'What's wrong?'

'There's a man in the garden.'

She tried to free her arm and suddenly he let go of her. She hurried across to the window and saw Conrad walking round to the gardening shed. 'It's only the old man who comes three times a week to do the gardening.'

'He'll be mowing the lawns and the mower's in the garage. He'll see the car. You want him to see the car's there, that's what. I told you what would happen if you tried to get help.'

She was completely bewildered by his fury.

'Stop him or I'll kill her. I'll kill her, just as I said I would.' He pushed her towards the pantry. 'Go on.'

She stumbled forward into the pantry and across to the outside door, which she unbolted.

'Call him here, d'you understand?' he said. 'Call him here and tell him to clear off.'

She opened the door. 'Tom,' she called out.

'Comin',' was the reply.

Krammer stepped back and half closed the door so that it concealed him.

Conrad came along the path, walking with the shuffling, toes-turned-out gait of a man who had spent the first twenty-five years of his working life plodding behind horses as they ploughed, harrowed, sowed, and reaped.

'What's up?' he asked in a surly voice. The wits of the village said that it was lucky he found work with her, since there was no one else barmy enough to employ him.

She tried to keep her voice level. 'There's no need for you to work here today.'

'What about them weeds in the taties-bed?'

'Never mind them.'

'I ain't 'avin' no convolvulations around me taties.'

'Leave them and come back Thursday.'

'What about me money?'

'You'll get it, just the same.'

'It be daft.'

'Never mind.'

'It be bluddy daft,' he said. He hawked noisily, turned his head to the right and spat. Then, muttering angrily to himself, shuffled along the path back to the gardening shed.

She stepped back into the pantry and Krammer shut the door and bolted it.

'I was terrified,' he said. 'If he'd found the car and told the police, and they'd come before the end of the four days, I'd be left without knowing. It has to be all of the four days because those other girls . . . I swear I didn't mean to hurt you.'

'It's all right.'

The smell of burning fat reached them and she hurried into the kitchen: blue smoke was rising from the frying-pan. She took it off the ring and turned down the gas under the saucepan of water.

'You're so brave,' he said. 'You're so different to everyone else. It makes me want to lie down on the ground and let you walk on me: I want you to hurt me because I want to suffer for you.'

'Please don't talk like that.'

'Why?'

'It sounds horrible, as if . . .' She stopped and got on with preparing breakfast. 'What about cereal?'

'She doesn't want any, Amelia.'

She put two eggs in the boiling water and broke two eggs into the frying-pan. When everything was ready and the boiled eggs were on the tray, Krammer picked it up.

'It's such fun watching her face when she sees what's on the tray,' he said. 'When she saw the tinned salmon she just couldn't believe it was all for her. I told her if she did eat it all she'd be sick, but she said she wouldn't. And she wasn't.'

'Please, when can I see her?'

'As soon as the four days are over, we'll go together. She's longing to meet you. It's like living with a miracle, Amelia. Can you possibly begin to realize what it'll be like when we both go up there and bring her down?'

'Of course.'

'I wonder whether you really can?'

.   .   .   .   .

At 12.28, at Palmersh General Hospital, a nurse went past the waiting detective, who was reading a paperback, and into the room in which was Chalmers. She looked down at his grey-white face and saw the sudden slight movement of his eyes. She left and went along the corridor to sister's office to report. When she returned to the room, to await the doctor, the detective spoke to her. 'Is he coming round?'

'He may be. I must go in and——'

'When can we talk to him?'

'Don't be so silly. It may be hours before he's really round.' She went into the room.

The detective hurried to the nearest telephone.

.   .   .   .   .

The two detectives waited outside the room, trying to control their impatience. At 3.17 in the afternoon they were told they could speak to Chalmers for a very short time. They went into the room and stood by the bed. Sister was at the head of the bed, belligerently determined to see her patient came to no harm.

'I'm Detective Inspector Agar,' said Agar, 'and this is another detective. We're wondering if you can tell us what happened?'

Speaking in short, sometimes disjointed, sentences, Chalmers told them what he remembered. The engine of the car had been going wrong and he had stopped in the middle of the common, climbed out, and had a look at the engine. Then the world exploded into blackness. That was all.

Agar stood upright. It was illogical to be so bitterly depressed by Chalmers' inability to help because from the beginning it had seemed certain it would be like this. But somewhere, in one of the corridors of his mind, had been the ridiculous, childish belief that Fate could never wholly abandon a young girl and that in the final event Chalmers would be able to help.

'Is that all?' asked Sister, in her harsh voice.

'That's all,' replied Agar.

'Then will you please leave.'

'Have I been able to help?' murmured Chalmers weakly.

'A little,' said Agar. He turned away from the bed.

'Anyway, he can't have gone far,' said Chalmers, as he shut his eyes.

Agar turned back. 'Why?' he snapped.

'Come along now,' said Sister. 'The doctor said . . .'

She stopped speaking as the door opened and the doctor came in. 'I've told them they must go,' she said.

'I'm sorry . . .' began the doctor.

'He's got to answer the question,' retorted Agar. He addressed Chalmers. 'Why couldn't he have gone far?'

Chalmers opened his eyes. 'I was running out of petrol and was going to get some at the all-night garage.'

The doctor went up to Agar's side. 'Out,' he snapped.

'How much petrol had you left?' asked Agar.

The doctor took hold of Agar's right arm.

'I was going to buy some at the all-night garage,' repeated Chalmers. 'I suppose there was a gallon left . . .' His voice trailed off and he closed his eyes.

The doctor pulled Agar away from the bed and then pushed him towards the door. Agar went out, followed by the doctor and Detective Sergeant Quorn.

'You're directly responsible for anything that happens to him,' said the doctor angrily, as soon as they were in the corridor.

'I had to know the answer,' replied Agar.

'You had no right to risk harming him. We know now we can do something for him: there's little chance anything can be done for her.'

Agar walked away. The doctor might be right or he might be wrong. All that was certain was that he, Agar, would have shaken the answers out of Chalmers if that had proved necessary.

.   .   .   .   .

The hastily convened conference was held at H.Q. and only the commander, who had returned to London that morning, was missing.

Pearce used a three-foot-long stick to indicate positions on the large map of the county which was hanging on the wall. 'Here's Stoneyacre. From the common, it's fourteen miles to Borley Woods and where Chalmers was dumped. We know Krammer called at this all-night garage and didn't buy any petrol. From the garage to Raleton is twenty-five miles and according to Chalmers there wasn't enough petrol in the tank to complete that journey. He had petrol left for twenty miles. Within a twenty-mile circle there are four all-night garages, at none of which did he call. We've asked the public to tell us if anyone gave him petrol Saturday night or had petrol syphoned out of their car, but we assume the answers to be negative. I'm going to assume one thing more. That Chalmers was right about the amount of petrol remaining so that there is this twenty-mile circle.'

'That cuts out Raleton,' said the A.C.C.

'Yes, sir.'

'What about the search there, then? It's a long way from being completed.'

'I recommend calling it off, sir.'

Everyone present knew the agony of the lonely decision which the assistant chief constable now had to make, a decision based on facts which might not be facts. What driver was certain to within a mere half-gallon how much petrol was left in his car's tank? An extra half-gallon in the Capri would have taken it to Raleton. If the centre of the search was shifted again, and later it was discovered that the girl had been, after all, in or near Raleton, the man who made the decision would find it difficult to live with himself.

There was silence in the room.

'Very well,' said the A.C.C. finally. 'Return searchers to this new circle and conduct a patterned search within it, concentrating initially on those areas which weren't covered by the first effort.'

There was one point no one had to make. The centre of the search had been shifted to Raleton when evidence of Krammer's visit to the London Road Garage had been uncovered. Had this not come to light and had the original search been completed, Sarah Bramswell might have been found by now. Evidence was more often than not ambiguous, which made it forever potentially tragic.

Mrs. Pretty and Krammer had dinner at 8.15. She had cooked the leg of lamb which was ordered the day before in an attempt to betray Krammer's presence in the house and she opened a bottle of Château Lafite, the last of five dozen that her late husband had bought nine months before his death.

Krammer sipped the wine and his studied attempt to appear to be a knowing connoisseur would, in a different context, have been ludicrously funny.

When he had finished eating he put his knife and fork carefully together in the centre of his plate. He spoke softly. 'This makes up for all my terrible unhappiness. Tomorrow night, when I'm reborn, I'll have so much to thank you for.'

'Why tomorrow?'

'It's the fourth day. By midnight tomorrow it will all be over.'

Fourteen

Agar walked away from the operations van, still parked in the middle of Stoneyacre Common. He went down the slight slope and then ten feet into the long grass, at which point he sat down. He lit a cigarette. The newly returned sunshine forced him to take off his coat.

It was Wednesday, 8.37 a.m., July the 21st. Sarah had now been missing for about eighty-one hours. That left fifteen hours to go. Not that ninety-six hours was a constant figure, accurate beyond doubt. Sarah would not die just as the clocks reached 11.15 p.m. But ninety-six had been the figure always before them and it left them only fifteen hours to go. Suppose they found Sarah now, would it be in time? Would he not already have so maimed her body and her mind that it was too late? He swore, repetitiously and without thinking. They had to find Sarah and it must not be too late.

What in the name of hell did they really have to go on? Take the twenty-mile circle. Accept the fact that at the beginning and after the first police appeal on the Sunday every loft, quarry, cave, outbuilding, or any other space which could possibly be a hiding place had been searched: then where could Krammer, Sarah, and the Ford be? The obvious answer was in a house, because only in a house with a garage could they obtain the complete cover they so obviously had. All those empty—and in south-east England there were very few—had been searched without results. Then was Krammer in an occupied house, terrorizing the occupants? This had been an obvious question from the beginning and every house had been visited by a policeman and the occupants questioned and not one police report had been positive. Since Sunday there had not been one report regarding suspicious behaviour which had proved to have any relevancy in it. Yet now they were as certain as they could be that Krammer was within the twenty-mile circle. Somewhere in that circle, then, there was a house where the occupants had tried to give the alarm and had been ignored despite the police's appeals. Before they knew of the twenty-mile circle, there had been no geographical location for this hypothetical house: now, it had to be close to.

Somewhere along the line, someone had missed something. It might have been the police, working under the terrible strain of the urgency of the case, or it might have been a member of the public who did not realize how slight might be the divergence from normal which would indicate Krammer's presence.

Where was Krammer most likely to be? Until recently, the answer must have been anywhere but in Stoneyacre. Krammer had driven away from there in a stolen car and it was known he reached the garage. But now that they 'knew' he hadn't reached Raleton, it was possible he had retraced his steps. He might even be in Stoneyacre, the one place where people presumed he couldn't possibly be.

Agar stood up and returned to the road, his jacket over his arm. He went into the operations van and spoke to the sergeant on duty. 'How many men are spare?'

'None, sir.'

'Then lay on half a dozen at once.'

'Can't be done, sir.'

'Goddamn it, don't argue. Just do it.'

159

'But . . .'

Agar left the van.

Half an hour later six uniformed policemen reported to the van. Agar addressed them. 'I want you to cover all villages between here and a line to the west of Torreton and Palmersh. You're to interview every shopkeeper, publican, vicar, postman, everyone who might be able to help, and you're to ask one simple question—does he or she know of anything that's happened which seems a little odd.'

One of the constables cleared his throat. 'That's already been done, I think, sir.'

'And now it's going to be done again.'

They became silent. Agar had a reputation for becoming a mean bastard when the pressure was on. Even if he was a busted D.C.I. who was never going to make the brass-hat country he was still a D.I. who outranked a pavement-basher.

'One final word,' said Agar. 'You're looking for a piece of evidence that will probably be so trivial the person who gives it to you will not know he is. So let the people talk on and on, even if it's only about Granny's pet corns. She may not have had corns until last Saturday night.'

      •   •   •   •   •

P.C. Jowett reported to Agar at 11.29 a.m. 'Sir,' he said, in his usual ponderous style, 'I have just completed my task in West Stoneyacre. I have interviewed all shopkeepers, the reverend vicar——'

'Get on with it,' snapped Agar.

'Very good, sir. One rag-and-bone man what always comes round on a Tuesday, but didn't this Tuesday.'

'Just making certain he keeps clear of us.'

Jowett looked up from the notebook. 'You did say, sir, it didn't matter how trivial.'

'All right. Now get on with it.'

'A man called Favour, sir, who did not get drunk on Saturday night which seems to be a record. Then a Mrs. Harmer was telephoning her cousin on Sunday morning and the wires got crossed and she heard two men talking about the killing they were going to make at Folkestone. She wondered if perhaps they weren't talking about the races, sir.'

'I can imagine.'

'And the butcher says that a Mrs. Pretty who lives at Adriadnoch House ordered a leg of lamb and three pounds of sausages and in the past fifteen years she's never had a joint or a single sausage.'

Agar felt as if an electric shock had suddenly jolted life into him. 'Hasn't she?'

The constable coughed. 'She's barmy, sir.'

'Who says?'

'Everyone, sir. She came here saying her husband had just died and she's hardly been out of the house since. They say she looks like the back of a bus. Her gardener is just as barmy.'

Agar lit yet another cigarette, even though his mouth already tasted like yesterday's incinerator. 'But she's never before been barmy enough to order sausages?'

'No, sir. As a matter of fact, there's the onions, too.'

'What onions?'

'She's never touched 'em before with a barge pole, wouldn't have any tins of anything with onions in them, but she ordered two pounds of onions on Monday.'

'Why the hell hasn't this been reported before?'

'They reckon she's just being a little bit barmier than usual, sir.'

Agar stood upright and stepped clear of his car against which he had been leaning. 'Who questioned Mrs. Pretty when Stoneyacre was covered on Sunday?'

'I don't know, sir. I'm from Palmersh.'

Agar ran across to the operations van. 'Find out who questioned Mrs. Pretty in Stoneyacre on Sunday,' he ordered.

'Yes, sir,' said the sergeant thickly, having almost been asleep.

'They're to contact me immediately.'

'Very good, sir.'

Agar returned to his car and ignored the waiting constable. Had Mrs. Pretty been desperately trying to tell people the truth and had she been totally ignored because people were so certain she was barmy? Or was she just plain barmy and that was the end of it? A case like Krammer's so often triggered off other mentally unstable people, as if all were suffering from a communicable disease. Did a leg of lamb, three pounds of pork sausages, and some onions really add up to anything?

The constable coughed. 'Well?' snapped Agar.

'There's one more point, sir.'

'What is it?'

'The vicar's wife, sir, mentioned that Mrs. Pretty rang her on Sunday to say that she couldn't arrange the flowers in the church on Sunday, but Mrs. Pretty never has done the flowers and the vicar's wife didn't know what she was talking about.'

'It must be,' said Agar. 'Why couldn't they have realized? Oh God, why couldn't they realize?'

There was a call from the van and the sergeant said he was wanted on the telephone.

Agar ran into the van and took the receiver. 'Agar speaking.'

'Sergeant Armstrong, sir. They said you wanted to speak with whoever called on Mrs. Pretty, sir.'

'Well?'

'I'm sorry, sir, I don't really know what it is you want to hear about?'

'What happened, man?'

'She was very abusive, sir, and told me to clear off and stop worrying her.'

'How abusive? Enough to make you wonder about it?'

'Not really, sir. She's been near as bad before when I've had to call on her. She acted as barmy that time as this.'

'Did you see her?'

'No, sir. The door was on a chain so I only saw a little bit of her.'

'Then there could easily have been someone standing behind her, threatening her?'

'Well, I . . . I suppose so, sir. If you put it like that, there could've been. But if I'd had any sort of suspicion, sir, I'd——'

'I know. Does she live on her own?'

'Yes, sir.'

'Is she on the telephone?'

'I think so, sir.'

'All right.' Agar replaced the receiver. If Krammer was in the house the police were going to have to move very carefully. The fact that Mrs. Pretty had not given the alarm more directly than she had must mean she was threatened too effectively to do so. The next move must obviously be to try to telephone her and leave her in a position where she could tell the police the truth merely be saying 'Yes'. There was just one more point he must clear up before telephoning—was there an extension in the house on which Krammer could listen? He rang the telephone exchange and put the question to them and after ten minutes they rang back and said there was no extension.

He put his hand on the telephone, but did not pick it up for a few seconds as he prayed silently that this was not another false lead occasioned by a woman who was mentally unstable.

He lifted the receiver and dialled. The ringing tone began. It went on. Wasn't she being allowed to answer? That could be just as definite.

Then the ringing was cut short in the middle of its ninth cycle and a woman's voice said: 'Yes?'

'This is Detective Inspector Agar of the county constabulary speaking. I've reason to believe Krammer may be there threatening you. If he is, just say yes and then go on to discuss the church fête.'

'No,' she answered, 'no one's in the house but me.'

He stared blankly through the window of the van. 'There's no one else in the house?'

'That's what I said.'

He had never known such a surge of bitter depression as now gripped him. It was an effort just to force himself to go on talking. 'Didn't you order a leg of lamb, some sausages, and some onions, although you never eat those things?'

'That's my business. What right have you to pry into my business?'

'And you told the vicar's wife on Sunday that you couldn't arrange the flowers in church?'

'I did.'

'But you never do arrange them.'

'This is sheer impertinence.'

'Why did you bother to ring up the vicar's wife and tell her you were not going to do something that you never had done?'

'Why shouldn't I?'

'You surely agree——'

'What I bother to do has nothing whatsoever to do with you.' She ended the call.

Agar slowly replaced the receiver. He felt completely emptied of emotion and he hated himself. Hadn't he yet been in the police force long enough to know that whilst two and two always made four, one could never be certain what was two.

The sergeant stared at Agar's face. 'Nothing, sir?'

'No.'

The sergeant cleared his throat and then spoke harshly. 'Not much time now, sir, not if it's like those other cases.'

Agar didn't answer, but left the van. He looked at his watch. It was lunchtime.

. . . . .

Mrs. Pretty passed Krammer the dish of potatoes. He took it from her with one hand and then placed his other hand momentarily on hers. 'Thank you,' he said. 'Thank you so much for not telling the police.' He smiled.

She answered him almost shyly. 'I knew what it would mean to you if they came here before the end of the four days. They're not the kind of people to understand.'

'I think you're the most wonderful person I've ever met.'

She felt herself blushing.

He put down the potato dish. He spoke in a low voice, never once looking away from her. 'Amelia, when it's all over, can I come along to see you?'

'No,' she said.

'Please.'

The pale blue eyes seemed to be hypnotizing her. Desperately, she looked away. Into her mind flashed the picture of herself trembling every time he touched her, of his coming into her bedroom, of her drawing his hand down on to her breast. She tried to remember her late husband, to gain strength from such memory, but the picture would not come and all she could think of was Krammer in her bedroom.

'You will let me, won't you, Amelia?'

'Yes,' she finally murmured, in a voice that shook.

.   .   .   .   .

Agar had lunch at home. He had little appetite.

'You're not eating enough to keep a sparrow alive,' said Caroline.

'I'm just not hungry.'

After a while she began to collect the plates together. 'When will they call the search off?'

'We'll keep on and on, but I suppose by tomorrow morning there won't be the same ghastly urgency. It'll just be a case of finding the body and Krammer and locking him away ready for the next time.'

She stood up. 'You'll have coffee, won't you?'

He looked at his watch.

'Whatever you think,' she said, 'you've the time. If you don't ease up a little you'll crack up.'

'It'll be time enough tomorrow.' He had spoken sharply and immediately recognized the fact. 'I'm sorry, Carry, I didn't mean to jump down your throat. But I was so certain I was right and now I feel as if I'd been drained of everything. D'you know, that bitch of a woman spoke to me as if I hadn't the right to question her! Doesn't she care about the kid?'

'Perhaps she's a lot madder than anyone thinks: she'd have to be not to worry about Sarah.'

'I was so certain I was right.'

'You've done your best, Bill.' They were, she knew, trite words, but they were none the less true. She left the dining-room and went into the kitchen where she made the coffee.

166

When she returned she found her husband had not moved but was still staring, a bitter expression on his face, down at the table.

As soon as the coffee was cool enough he drank it and then stood up and kissed her good-bye.

He drove through Carriford to the London road and south to Stoneyacre. He parked behind the operations van and went inside where he met Raydon.

'Anything?' he asked, without hope.

'Not a bloody thing.'

With nothing more definite to do, Agar gave Raydon a hand checking the field operations of the close-patterned search, making certain from the maps that no piece of countryside was left out.

The heat in the van was oppressive and they became so sleepy that frequently they had to stand up and walk a few times up and down the length of the van to try to drive away a little of their sleepiness.

At 4.08 p.m. one of the three telephones rang. Agar reached across the table and picked it up. 'Agar speaking.'

'It's P.C. Vernon, sir.'

'Who?'

'Vernon, sir. I'm one of the six men you sent out this morning.'

Good God! thought Agar, the six policemen were still going round the countryside. In his bitter disappointment and tiredness he had completely forgotten them.

Vernon made his report. 'I've just had a word with one of the local postmen, sir. The only thing he knows happened on Monday morning, sir, and as he says it doesn't add up to anything, but like you said——'

'Get on with it, man.'

'Yes, sir. Well, he went to this house and was about to deliver the letters when the door opened and the woman

167

stood there. He says she almost gave him a turn, she looked so queer. Then she opened her mouth like she was going to speak, but there was a quiet cough and she kept mum. He asked her if something was wrong and she said there weren't nothing. He made some remarks about the weather, but she wasn't in a talking mood, so he gave her the letters and left. He says he's been four years on that round and it's the first time he's ever laid eyes on her and she's a real odd one.'

'What house?' asked Agar, excitement once more flaming up in his mind.

'Adriadnoch House, sir. She's a Mrs. Pretty.'

'Vernon, this is vitally important. Can you get hold of the postman for me?'

'I thought it could be you'd want a word with him, sir, so I've got him waiting outside this call-box. I'll get him.'

There was a pause, then a man said: 'You want a word with me?'

'I do indeed, and thanks for helping. Will you describe everything to me as exactly as you can remember it?'

'Well, it's like this. I drives up and parks the van and goes to the front door. I'm about to shove the letters into the letter-box when the door opens and I'm left holding them out like a right proper Charlie. It's a woman and she looks like she's just trod on a snake. She opens her mouth to speak and then there's this cough and she shuts her mouth quicker than quick. I asks her if something's the matter and she says nothing. It doesn't seem she likes chatting, so I goes.

'Mister, if I'd thought there was anything to this, I'd've told someone, but they'd told me long ago how she was barmy, like.'

The terrible tragedy of a reputation, thought Agar. 'Could she have been the one to cough?' he asked.

'It wasn't her. That's for sure.'

'What kind of cough was it?'

'Just a cough. Quiet like, and kind of polite.'

'Was it a man or a woman?'

'Well, I don't rightly know.'

'Care to guess?'

'I suppose I'd say it was a man.'

'Thanks very much.'

'Mister,' said the postman hurriedly, 'you've got to believe me that I didn't think anything of it. Until the policeman spoke to me——'

Agar impatiently cut him short. 'I know. Thanks.' He rang off.

'Something?' asked Raydon.

'It's got to be, it's bloody well got to be.' But he remembered how Mrs. Pretty had denied Krammer was with her at a time when she could have said he was without any danger to herself.

'What is it?' asked Raydon, watching Agar's face.

'I don't know. Why? Why did she deny it over the phone? If she's just plain barmy, who coughed? Look, Don, this is the way it goes.' Succinctly, he gave Raydon the facts.

At the end Raydon looked troubled. 'But if Krammer were there she must have told you so over the phone.'

'Yet I'm sure of it.'

'What are you going to do?'

'Search the house.'

'But on what she's already said to you she's bound to refuse to let you in.'

'I'll get a search warrant.'

'And if you're refused one?'

Agar shook his head and made no answer.

Fifteen

Agar left the J.P.'s house and stood on the pavement, staring at the two waiting police cars. The search warrant had been refused by an elderly J.P., who withered, dithered, and waffled on about insufficient evidence. So what did he do? He went to the leading car.

'All right, sir?' asked the driver.

To act without a warrant was to commit professional suicide if Krammer was not in the house. But he knew that he dare not take the risk, however great it was. 'Stop asking questions,' he snapped, 'and get the bloody car moving.'

They drove the eight miles to Stoneyacre at speeds which were sometimes as high as ninety. Both cars came to a halt a hundred yards from the drive leading up to Adriadnoch House. Agar climbed out and stood on the pavement. Once more his mind reminded him of the risks and once more, inevitably, there could be no question of what he was going to do. He turned and walked to the second car. 'You three out and round to the back of the house. The belt of trees will give you some cover. Take up positions and if I give the signal break in wherever it's easiest. If there's no signal after ten minutes come round to the front.'

'Right, sir,' said Sergeant Quorn, as he stepped out of the car. He pushed his way through a narrow gap in the blackthorn hedge.

Agar returned to the leading car. The driver engaged first gear and they went forward and down the drive, coming to a halt in front of the rather ugly old rectory.

He climbed out, crossed to the front door, and knocked. The iron knocker, in the shape of a cockerel's head, gave a thudding sound which seemed to echo. He shivered as a sense of evil gripped him. He jeered at himself, saying that his imagination had taken leave of his senses. He looked at his wristwatch. It was 4.59—4.59 on the afternoon of the fourth day.

He knocked again, several times.

The door opened about six inches, held from moving any further by a chain. 'What do you want?' demanded a woman, her voice shrill.

'My name is Detective Inspector Agar. I have reason to believe an escaped prisoner, George Krammer, is somewhere inside the house. May I come in, please?'

'There's no one here. Go away.'

He became certain she was lying. But even at this moment of tense, fearful excitement one question worried him more than any other: why? 'Do you let us in or do we have to break in, Mrs. Pretty?'

'You can't do that. Go away. Go away,' she shouted.

He raised his right hand and the uniformed constable at the corner of the house did the same. Seconds later he heard the drawn-out sound of breaking glass. Then he seemed to hear the woman moaning, as if in pain.

The wait seemed to last an eternity. Wildly, he wondered what in the name of hell his men were doing. Then she screamed and there was some sort of scuffle, after which the front door was closed until the chain could be withdrawn. The door was opened and he stepped inside.

He stared at the woman and was struck first by how ugly she was and then by the expression of deep tragedy on her face.

'Why couldn't you wait?' she demanded wildly.

He looked past her. 'Where is he?'

She began to cry. 'Why couldn't you have waited? Now you've destroyed him.'

She really was barmy, thought Agar suddenly, and he felt chilled by the knowledge of what that meant. All her past actions were without meaning and he had read into them things that were not there. He felt sick: not because of the trouble he was now in, but because he was no nearer Sarah Bramswell.

Suddenly the door on the left was flung open and a man came out into the hall. He was of medium height, well dressed in a blazer and grey flannels, and he had pale blue eyes. He held a revolver in his right hand.

Agar stared at Krammer, hating him. Any relief at finding him at last, any fear at being threatened by a gun, was completely lost in this surge of overwhelming hate. 'Put that gun down,' he said.

Krammer cocked the revolver and there was a loud click as he brought the hammer back with his thumb.

A constable, previously out of sight of Krammer, began to move slowly and carefully forward.

'Put that gun down, Krammer,' said Agar, trying to draw all of Krammer's attention. 'You can't get away and it'll do you no good.'

'Look out,' shouted Mrs. Pretty wildly. 'There's a man behind you.'

Krammer instinctively turned to his left. Quorn, who was nearest, threw himself forward and crashed into Krammer's side, knocking him off balance and against the wall. Agar ran and grabbed Krammer's wrist and twisted it so savagely that he instantly dropped the gun. Quorn slammed his fists twice into Krammer's face, Agar jerked his right knee up and there was a shrill drawn-out scream. A constable began to hit Krammer: one, two, one, two, as if he were a punchbag. Quorn went on hammering Krammer's face.

'That's enough,' said Agar, after a while.

Quorn and the constable stopped, hesitated, and then moved back, expressions almost of bewilderment on their faces.

Krammer had collapsed, unconscious, on to the floor. Blood flowed from his nose and mouth and his ear looked torn.

'You've killed him,' cried Mrs. Pretty.

'Resisting arrest,' said Agar.

'He was only trying to escape. If you hadn't . . .'

'Resisting arrest,' said Quorn hoarsely.

She knelt down by the unconscious man and cradled his head in her lap, careless of the blood which soaked into her cotton frock. Tears rolled down her cheeks. 'You've destroyed him. You've destroyed his soul.'

Agar spoke roughly. 'Where's the girl?'

She ignored his question. 'He was trying to find himself and now you've destroyed him. Why did you have to come so soon?'

'The girl?' shouted Agar.

'He looked after her as if he were her own father.' She began to try to wipe some of the blood off Krammer's face with a lace-edged handkerchief. 'He served her, gave her the things she liked. The more he served her, the more wonderful it was for him. Yet you had to come and destroy him.'

'Are you saying the girl's unhurt?' asked Agar, almost whispering.

She looked up. 'Yes.'

'Thank God,' he murmured, and the rush of relief was so great that his eyes watered. When he looked at the nearest constable, he saw that he was not the only one to react like this. 'Thank God,' he said for the second time.

After a while he spoke to her again. 'Where is she?' He

looked away from the bloody, unconscious Krammer and the ugly woman whose raw and naked emotion was an embarrassing thing to see. 'Which room is she in?'

'Upstairs,' she replied. 'It's locked and he's got the key.'

He did not try to understand all her emotions, but he did know that here was some tragedy almost as great as the one that had been averted. 'Check his pockets,' he ordered.

Mrs. Pretty waved aside Quorn and carefully searched the blazer pockets. She brought out a key, which she handed in silence to Agar.

Agar ordered two of the men to carry the unconscious Krammer to somewhere safe and then he told Quorn to accompany him upstairs. As he walked to the stairs he remembered the expression he had last seen on the Bramswells' faces and the knowledge that he would be able to wipe away all that ghastly agony gave him a spiritual uplift such as he had never before believed possible.

He and Quorn went up, past the half-landing with the bare patch in the carpet, to the bedrooms.

Almost opposite them as they reached the top was an open door, showing part of a barely furnished bedroom. To their left was a closed door and to their right, along the dim passage, were several more closed doors. He tried the left-hand door first and this was unlocked: the room was obviously Mrs. Pretty's. He turned, passed the stairs, and found that the second door on the left was locked. He put the key into the lock, turned it, and there was a click. He opened the door.

He stared at the bed and the girl who lay on it, gagged and bound. He thought he was going to be sick. He looked at Quorn and saw the same expression that he knew must be on his face. He looked back at the bed and the girl moved and for the first time he realized she was still alive.

'Call the doctor,' he ordered, his voice little more than a croak. 'Tell H.Q.'

Quorn turned and ran down the stairs. There was the noise of a number of voices which suddenly died away.

Agar had to force himself to go into the room. He passed a pile of food which had been dumped on the floor and much of which had gone bad. Flies were everywhere. Near the food was a jumble of old-fashioned books.

He took the gag out of the girl's mouth and cut the bonds. He covered her naked body with a sheet. As the gag was taken from her mouth, she moaned, but did not open her eyes.

He found his hands were trembling and he thrust them into his trousers pockets. There was a sound from behind and he turned. Mrs. Pretty stood in the doorway.

'She's all right, isn't she? That policeman was lying?' she said shrilly.

He made no reply.

A buzzing bluebottle caught her attention and drew it to the heap of rotting food. She stared with disbelief at the food. 'What . . . what happened?' she whispered.

He shook his head.

She came into the room and crossed to the bed. She put out her right hand and took hold of the sheet.

'Don't,' he said.

She pulled the sheet back. She stared down at the girl for several seconds, then replaced the sheet. She stepped back and her heel kicked one of the books. 'He told me she had asked for something to read and I chose those specially,' she said.

'Why not leave?'

'He told me she was sleeping with her hair spread all round her face so that she looked like an angel. I believed him. Do you understand? I believed him. He told me how she liked her eggs and I prepared them for her exactly as he said she wanted them. When he brought the tray down after that breakfast there was only half a slice of bread and butter left. I was certain she must be all right. He used to tell me what she specially liked to eat and I prepared it for her. That's why she had the tinned salmon, there. And the lemon meringue pie, there. I asked to see her and we went upstairs together and knocked on the door and when there wasn't an answer he looked inside quickly and said she was still asleep. Yet all the time, she was . . . she was . . .'

'Let's go out,' said Agar.

Despair, grief, and hatred made her uglier than ever. 'But you've got to know.'

'Why not wait to tell it?'

'He was lying all the time. He told me all those lies to get extra pleasure from what he was doing to her. He was jeering at me. . . .'

'Never forget one thing,' he said quietly. 'If he hadn't . . . done as he did, Sarah would probably have been dead by now. This is near the end of the fourth day. But because of you he didn't start as soon as he would otherwise have done.'

She had apparently not heard him. 'He mocked me. He said my name reminded him of blossom in the spring. That's what my late husband used to say. I believed him. Then he came . . . to my bedroom.'

Agar walked to the door, trying to escape her words.

'He came into my bedroom and I wanted him. That's what happened. I wanted him. I wanted him so much I believed him and when there was a telephone call, I said he wasn't here. If I'd told the truth then . . .'

He left the room.

* * * * *

Charles Bramswell ran up the drive to the front door of Adriadnoch House. The uniformed constable said he couldn't go in and he wildly tried to push past.

'Now then, sir . . .'

Agar, in the hall, saw the struggle and called out. The constable let go of Bramswell.

'Sarah?' cried Bramswell, as he came up to Agar. 'You've got to tell me. In the village they said there were police here and it must be to do with Sarah. Is she here?'

Bitterly, Agar knew that he was not to be allowed to escape any of the frightful cruelty of the aftermath of this case. 'She's here,' he said.

'Alive?'

'Yes, but injured.'

'How badly?'

'The doctor has seen her and treated her and called for an ambulance. It's not as bad as it could have been.'

Bramswell closed his eyes for a few seconds, then he opened them. 'I want to see her.'

'Wait until she's been in the hospital for a bit.'

'I want to see her. It might not be Sarah.'

'It is Sarah.'

'I must see her.'

Agar turned and indicated the stairs. They went up and along to the door of the bedroom. The constable who was standing there looked at Agar and opened the door.

'She's under very heavy sedation,' said Agar.

They went in and over to the bed. Bramswell looked down at Sarah's head and watched her barely perceptible breathing. He took hold of the sheet.

Agar hesitated, but finally said nothing.

Bramswell pulled the sheet back. 'That's Sarah.' He replaced the sheet, looked straight at Agar, suddenly turned and ran out of the room.

Agar lit another cigarette. Tomorrow people would read about this in the newspapers and would be vicariously, but only temporarily, shocked: if only they could be brought here to see what crime really meant.

He leaned against the wall and drew smoke into his lungs. How many people's lives had been ruined by Krammer? Dozens or hundreds? Charles, Betty, Sarah Bramswell, and Mrs. Pretty were only the latest four.

He heard the sound of voices downstairs and recognized one of them. He left the room and went to the head of the stairs. By leaning over the banisters he could see the assistant chief constable. Reluctantly he went down the stairs.

With the assistant chief constable were the commander, Detective Superintendent Pearce, and Detective Inspector Raydon.

'Where is she?' asked Pearce.

'Upstairs, sir, second door to the right.'

'What did the doctor say?'

'He's not prepared to do more than say she'll live, sir. There's no knowing how badly her mind has been shocked. He said the hospital will try that new drug which destroys memory.'

'Is the ambulance on its way?'

'Yes, sir.'

'We'll go up now.'

They climbed the stairs, four men whose movements suggested they would rather do anything than reach the end of their journey.

Quorn came up to Agar. 'What about the Press, sir?'

'We'll let the super handle that problem.'

'They're getting very restive.'

'They'll keep.'

'Yes, sir.' Quorn looked quickly at Agar, then away.

When he spoke the tone of his voice was neutral. 'How's Krammer, sir? Has he recovered consciousness yet?'

Agar ignored the question. 'Kim, how d'you begin to make sense of a man like Krammer? Can *you* even begin to climb into the mind of a man who can do that to a girl of twelve? How any human can do what he did to Mrs. Pretty because he got extra pleasure from it . . .' He did not finish.

'What did he do to her, sir?'

'Let's leave it.'

'Yes, sir,' said Quorn, uncomfortably, hating anything which threatened to stir his imagination from the state of stunned incomprehension it was in. 'I don't suppose you saw the old girl after she left the room?'

'No.'

'She looked as sick as the poor bastard of a father did just now.'

Agar stubbed out his cigarette on the sole of his shoe. 'I wonder if she'll be able to live with herself again?'

'Yes, sir,' said Quorn, and his answer had no meaning. 'What about Krammer, sir?'

'I suppose I'd better go and see if he's recovered consciousness yet.'

'Did the Doc look him over, sir?'

'I didn't suggest it.'

'No, sir.'

'Has anyone told you where Krammer was taken to?'

'The pantry. There aren't any windows and the inside door locks and bolts on the kitchen side.'

Agar found out where the pantry was and walked along the corridor, past the door anachronistically covered with green baize, and into the kitchen. He crossed to the pantry door and withdrew the bolts, then turned the key and pulled the door open. For the first two steps his view was restricted by the rows of shelves on his left, then his third step took him clear of them and he saw Krammer.

Krammer was hanging from the ceiling by a length of rope taken through one of the bacon hooks in the roof and made fast to a metal bar set in the wall.

Agar looked for the chair on which Krammer must have stood in order to commit suicide. There was no chair. Nor was the table near enough for him to have used that as his launching platform.

There was an old wooden chair in the far corner and Agar brought this to the centre of the room and set it down immediately to one side of the gently swaying body. He stood on the chair and examined the length of rope between the hook in the ceiling and the steel bar set in the wall. On one side of the rope, but not constantly on the same side because the rope had revolved, the fibres were all turned upwards, towards the ceiling. That meant the rope had been pulled over the hook. Krammer had never recovered consciousness and committed suicide. Probably, someone had come in and tried to hang Krammer by putting his head through the noose, already in position: the weight of the unconscious man had been too great. That person had then slacked the rope away until the noose could be fitted over Krammer's head and he could be hauled up.

Agar hesitated for a while. A sound from the doorway made him turn suddenly, but there was no one there. He quickly ran his hand along the fibres of the rope, forcing them into a hotchpotch of angles. He climbed down from the chair and pushed it over.

·　　·　　·　　·　　·

The assistant chief constable stood to one side of the pantry and watched the men place Krammer's body on a stretcher, cover it with a sheet, and carry it out. He looked across the room, first at Pearce and then at Agar. 'Agar.'

'Sir?'

'What's the truth?'

An expression of angry annoyance momentarily crossed Pearce's face.

'The truth, sir?' asked Agar, as if he could not understand the question.

'Look, man, it's no good treating me like a bloody fool. I don't have to be a genius to know just how hard you and the others hit Krammer when you first found him. Maybe I'd have hit even harder. But this is different. Krammer was brought in here unconscious—and that's how he remained. When you came in you found him swinging from the hook and you had a good look at things. You damn' soon saw he'd been hauled up there, didn't you?'

'No, sir.'

'If he was hanged someone's got to be charged with his murder. You know that as well as I do. It's murder to kill a murderer.'

'So the law says, sir.'

'And you're part of the law and not outside or beyond it. Where was this chair?'

'Where it is now, sir.'

'Whose fingerprints will be found on it?'

'Mine, apart from anyone else's, sir.'

'Because you moved it under the body.'

'Because I almost tripped over it, sir, and had to grab hold of it for support.'

'How did you come to trip over it?'

'Through rushing to the body, sir, to see if there was any life left.'

'Why didn't you let the rope down instead of cutting it?'

'It would have been evidence, sir, had anyone murdered him by hauling him up from the ground.'

The A.C.C.'s voice became angrier. 'The fibres of the rope are pointing all over the place.'

'Yes, I noticed that, sir.'

'How were they originally?'

'Just as you found them, sir.'

'You're a liar, Agar. Your past record tells me that. You beat up a man once, remember?'

'I'm hardly likely to forget, sir.'

'Then why d'you go on trying to make out you've forgotten? You're a policeman, nothing more. You're not the judge and you're not the jury. The government said that Krammer had as much right to go on living as you have, whether he killed one or ten girls. So that meant Sarah Bramswell suffered. That's nothing to do with you.'

'Some people might agree with you, sir.'

'Agar, admit the truth now and I'll personally guarantee we'll do what we can to hush up your attempt to hide Krammer's murder. Damn it all, man, d'you think I like it any more than you? D'you think I wouldn't have hoisted him up myself? But there's the law to do the punishing.'

'And it failed, didn't it?'

'This is my last warning. No matter what my own feelings are, and I'm not saying, I can't not give orders for investigations to be made into Krammer's hanging. Medical evidence will tell whether he was conscious or unconscious when he was hanged. You can't escape the pathologist's report.'

'I've been telling the truth, sir.'

'You leave me without any option,' said the A.C.C. harshly.

•   •   •   •   •

Agar walked up and down the tiled room off which was the morgue. He paused to light one cigarette from the burning stub of another and then went on pacing. Detective Superintendent Pearce, slumped in one of the hard-backed chairs, watched him.

The door opened and the pathologist came just inside the ante-room. He began to peel off the rubber gloves he was wearing.

'Well, sir?' said Pearce, as he came to his feet.

The pathologist looked at him for several seconds.

'Impossible to tell,' he finally said, his Scottish accent very strong.

Pearce spoke slowly. 'The A.C.C. seemed to think you'd be able to judge without trouble, sir.'

'Then you'll be able to inform him that he thought wrong.'

'Yes, sir.'

'All right, gentleman, that's all. I'll bid you good-bye.' He returned the way he had come.

Agar and Pearce went out into the sunshine.

'I'll make out the report,' said Pearce. 'I've always maintained the Scots are a logical race. Bill, we need a pint to try to wash some of the taste out of our mouths.' They walked to the edge of the pavement and waited for traffic to thin out sufficiently for them to cross the road. 'Would you call Mrs. Pretty a physically strong woman, Bill?'

'Reasonably so.'

'But not quite as strong as Bramswell?'

'I hadn't thought about it.'

A lorry went past them and they were able to hurry across the road to the public house, immediately opposite.

Caroline was waiting in the sitting-room, her face showing the heavy strain of wondering and fearing. Agar went into the room.

'Well?' she asked, her voice high.

'The P.M. showed nothing.'

'But . . . but you said it was certain it would.'

'The pathologist was a Scotsman.'

'I don't understand, Bill.'

'As Pearce said earlier on, the Scots are a very logical race.' He went forward and took her hand in his. 'Would you leave it at that, Carry?'

She gripped his hand tightly and was content to know she would never learn the whole truth.